Geoffrey M Bould

This book is a work of fiction and characters and names are the product of the author's imagination. Any resemblance to real persons, living or dead, is coincidental.

Geoffrey Boult has asserted his right under the Copyright, Designs and Patents Act 1988 to be identified as the author of this work.

ISBN 978-0-9531518-1-3

Published by MilesBradenford Publishing, Arlesey, Beds

June 2016

Species Hs53

By

Acknowledgments

I am most grateful to family and friends for their support and constructive comments during the writing of this book;

Ruth & Simon, Zoe, Roger

Michael, Maggie, Debbie, Kay, Rob, Christine

and especially to Christine for proof-reading.

Chapter 1

Gerry had no way of knowing that on this sunny, warm Wednesday he would wake up for the last time a free man.

It was August and some of the leaves on the trees of the Smithsonian National Zoo were beginning to turn, just as they had done for countless years before. Gerry had worked at the zoo all his working life, since he completed his doctorate at Harvard. He had a first in Organismic and Evolutionary Zoology. He was considered a high flyer and had been offered several lectureships at prestigious universities both in the States and Europe. He had a scholarly attitude. Logic and proper argument were paramount to him. Emotions had to learn to take a back seat in his life.

Yet academia wasn't for him. He loved the hands-on business of examining different animal species, especially the apes. It was in his relationship with them that his emotions were allowed a brief outing.

From his appearance you might have thought he was a doctoral student, rather than a Doctor. His wavy ginger hair seldom engaged in combat with scissors. His pale face was dominated by a somewhat random growth of beard and his clothing indicated that he found his physical appearance to be of no concern. He wasn't indifferent to the need to be clean but beyond that he was irritated by anything that got in the way of his work.

Fortunately for everyone his temperament was even, perhaps tolerant. Although indifferent might be a more accurate description.

Anyway, the opinions of universities these days were of somewhat insignificant importance. They were still allowed their autonomy, to a degree. But the real business was happening elsewhere.

He used his electric car to come to work as usual. It was parked in the parking lot as usual. He peered into the retinal scan device at the entrance to the Zoo as usual. And as usual he was admitted to the complex, through the heavy lead-lined steel doors. Had he been looking in the right direction, what Gerry might have noticed as being out of the normal run of things was that his car un-parked itself and calmly drove itself out of the parking lot and away down the highway. Vehicle A274j had been re-assigned. Gerry wouldn't be needing it any more.

The Hub was where it was all happening. The Hub wasn't a place; it wasn't really any identifiable object. It was more of a concept. The best description would be that it was a computer. But its hardware was distributed all over the Western Nations. It was the aggregate of individual systems in houses and offices; and of all the microscopic computers in goods ranging from fridges to cars, pens to crisp packets. It included the ID chips in dogs and cats and other creatures – including humans. It included the plethora of robot operatives that carried out mundane activities. Just about everything had a tiny computer in it; and they were all connected to the central Hub.

That Hub would collect and aggregate data from these billions of chips and, acting as a massive neural network, would identify patterns and resonances throughout the Western Atlantic Nations.

The Hub routinely received DNA samples from all university graduates, post-graduates and doctorates, but it also received the same data stream from road sweepers, cleaners and prostitutes. In fact there wasn't a single walk of life that the Hub wasn't concerned with.

For the Hub, Gerry's employment at the Smithsonian Zoo was fortunate, since it coincided with the result of the combination of Prime Directive 247 and his particular DNA.

At 3 o'clock that morning, the Hub had combined the data and the directive and issued an instruction that would seal Gerry's fate. At first Gerry didn't notice a thing.

Of course, once inside the building, he could not see the parking lot. The entire environment of the zoo was artificially controlled. It was built on a thick foundation of reinforced concrete, also lead lined. The atmosphere was synthesised from a vast reserve of chemicals. The oxygen and CO_2 levels were mainly moderated by the plant and animal life of the zoo, though sophisticated processes were used to clean it up or restore the correct balance from time to time.

On the face of it, if you didn't know it was a zoo, you might have thought of it as a vast nuclear bunker. That's what workers there called it – the bunker. Though they knew of course that it was the requirements of scientific rigour that demanded complete isolation from the outside world. And – hey! It's always a perfect temperature and humidity inside, so who's going to complain?

At about the same time an apartment in Irving Street NW suddenly appeared on the vacancies list. It was a first floor apartment with a good view of the street. Its furnishings were precisely suited to the preferences of its previous occupant. Its atmosphere was clean and crisp, its contents meticulously ordered and everything put away in its proper place. Within an hour it had been re-assigned to another person, Avril Parkinson.

Avril worked in law, was 32, not involved and had been on the waiting list for a property in Columbia Heights for several weeks. She was average height, slim with boyish hips and long brown hair. As a child she had been blonde and vivacious. As an adult she had become quiet and reserved. Not so much from self-consciousness or timidity but as a result of an inner confidence which meant she felt no need to speak unless there was a very good reason.

Some men felt her to be mysterious and a little frightening. She just believed herself to be ordinary and of little consequence. In this matter they were right and she was wrong. That evening a removal truck would appear outside her current apartment; removal operatives would appear and stow all her stuff and, very swiftly and efficiently, all her worldly goods would be moved into Gerry's old place. At the same time another similar vehicle would appear outside Gerry's place and operatives would swiftly remove all his belongings and pack them in the van. Since the operatives never tired and had limitless patience they would approach each item with identical efficiency, even down to the last paper-clip. When they had finished the vehicle would drive itself away to the zoo. Gerry's possessions would carefully be moved into his new apartment. Gerry had no idea of the drama that was about to be played out in his life.

The Western Atlantic Nations had itself grown out of the North Atlantic Treaty Organisation but now included the South American countries, the whole of Africa, Australasia and all the European States to the west of a line drawn roughly from the northern tip of Finland to the Suez. People who lived in that region, including Gerry, considered it to be the *civilised world* - simply because just about everybody and everything in that region was connected to the central Hub. For short it was known as the West. The remainder of the planet was rather dismissively referred to as "The East." The East lived under a cloud of fear – fear of the Chinese and Russian super powers, but also fear of the West. Thus the whole interconnected system of the West, which acted as though it had an intelligence of its own, went by the name of The Hub.

Although the East was catching up in terms of technology, it did not have such a saturation of chips in every piece of technology and it had nothing to match the Hub.

The Hub had a range of criteria it applied in sifting its universally large mass of data and ironically Gerry's intellectual ability currently did not rate. Something much more basic and academically more interesting was what the Hub noticed in Gerry.

The Hub noticed everything – well everything that mattered. It had a set of Prime Directives – a set of inalienable rules. They provided the moral basis on which it made its decision. They protected the sanctity of human life and defined the bounds within which that sanctity applied. They defined the boundaries of socially acceptable behaviour. They encapsulated the laws that were formerly the business of the courts and they protected the diversity of genetic material in the civilised world.

He found his way to his office by the usual route, doors opening automatically as they sensed the emissions of the chip implanted in the back of his neck. Gerry's move had resulted from his DNA profile. Avril's move was the fortunate consequence. The Hub had not reviewed Avril's DNA for some time now and might never do so. Some samples were not considered to be interesting or unique enough to warrant review.

The chip in Gerry's neck played no significant part in his conscious life. He knew it was there – it had been there since before he was born. Normally they were implanted at about 4-5 months gestation. Everyone who was anyone had one. And all the routine transactions of life – ordering a vehicle, getting into buildings, acquiring goods, food etc. – all of these mundane activities were processed by the unperceivable exchange of data between his chip and the System. The chip also monitored its host's vital signs – pulse, temperature, blood pressure and so on.

Some decades before there had been objections to the universal implantation of PIDACs – Personal ID and Controller chips. The "Internet of Things" had been an earlier revolution and no one turned a hair at their fridge automatically ordering bacon and egg when stocks got low. Now such technology was universal.

However when the same technology was trialled in humans, the cry from the human rights organisations had been "Are we just *things* as well now?" A pertinent if tardy question.

By the time Gerry was born, anyone expressing such insurrectionist views would have their PIDAC deactivated. There was no formal punishment for such anti-social behaviour. There didn't need to be. You were just isolated from all services. You could sleep rough if you wanted to. But you wouldn't survive for long. In any case there were always two doors still open to you – quite literally. These doors led off the waiting room in any of the civil centres, dotted around the towns and cities. You could choose to be re-commissioned, go through a re-training programme and have your chip re-activated. Or you could go through the termination door. Not many people did. Not for that reason anyway. Unsurprisingly those people whose PIDACs had been deactivated were often referred to as the 'walking dead.' More often as '*deacts*'.

So, Gerry, being an upstanding member of society, without any record of unsocial behaviour, had no problem accessing all the services that he needed. That is, until today, Wednesday.

Gerry was quite unaware of the change his life was about to experience, until lunch-time. Normally he would head down the corridor, out into the entrance lobby and have a short walk around the surrounding park. This day, however, he found the door from the corridor into the entrance lobby would no longer open for him. There was no angry alarm sound. No judgemental synthesised voice barking "Access Denied!" Instead a very calm, though still synthesised voice spoke kindly;

"I'm sorry Gerry, you can't use this door just now."

Gerry wasn't particularly worried. Partly because he didn't get worried easily. Partly because there were other doors and often a particular route would be closed off for maintenance or cleaning purposes. Such protocols made health and safety a routine matter, not an extra consideration. If you could open a door, you knew it would be safe to go through it. Gerry tried another door at the other end of the corridor but with the same result. And a third. Then he realised that the only remaining door was the one back into his office area.

Then, and only then, it began to dawn on him.

Chapter 2

Avril left her day's work a little tired but very excited. As she left her office she wore the faintest sign of a smile. Most people wouldn't have noticed it but Mary, her longest standing colleague and possibly a friend, did.

"You're looking happy today!"

Avril gave her a sheepish grin and raised her eyebrows. Mary knew there was no point in pressing for more information. From experience she knew that it would take a considerable quantity of alcohol to breach Avril's defences. At last she was moving into her new apartment. She had left her old one only a few hours ago and now was being transported by her car to her new pad. The system had automatically updated her PIDAC with her new address, which in turn was directing the car to its new location. Avril arrived on the threshold of her apartment just moments after the operatives had left.

There was a welcome card on the table along with a bottle of wine. She thought it was strange how centuries of scientific advance had made driving redundant, yet bottles were still the preferred method of delivering wine. She picked up the bottle and inspected the label. It seemed to be of reasonable quality. She was looking forward to trying it later.

The operatives had also made her bed, arranged her furniture just as she liked it, stocked the cupboards and fridge with her selected range of items and set the environmental controls to the precise recipe that she liked at this time of the year. She knew nothing about the previous occupant. There were no residues. Cleaner operatives had dowsed everything with a highly toxic but short lived chemical, so that the whole place was shiny clean and smelt of roses. The aroma of roses was Avril's favourite perfume. As Avril had walked in, the door automatically identifying and recognising her, she had inhaled slowly, enjoying the familiar scent of her favourite rose.

14

Although it was exactly the same specification as the one in her previous apartment, there are always subtle microscopic differences about a building that can't be erased. They contribute a little something to the overall odour and Avril's keen sense of smell was able to detect just that subtle variation. Subtle variations were meat and drink to the Hub.

One of its Prime Directives related to the discovery and preservation of variations in the DNA of different species of animal. The Hub's vast worldwide database kept records of the association of these variations with differences in appearance and behaviour. The Hub, through the World Genetic Bank, controlled over 10,000 zoos across the planet, monitoring the environments of the various specimens, their health, oxygen or CO_2 output and consumption. Operatives would take readings and samples where necessary but much of it was done automatically.

The background had been the cataclysmic events of the end of the 21st century. Human beings had proved themselves to be brilliant at innovation and experiment; but next to useless at anticipating and controlling the negative effects of their endeavours. By the end of the century hundreds of thousands of species of animal, plant and insect had become extinct.

All the major governments of the West had eventually, and rather too late, organised themselves to capture and maintain examples of all the remaining species – the Noah project. They had set up a trans-national organisation, the World Genetic Bank (WGB), to catalogue the species and define protocols for preserving them. The result of this massive piece of international administrative cooperation was the compulsory acquisition of all zoos across the West. In order to direct the actions of this vast array of institutions, the WGB formulated a set of Prime Directives which would act as the foundation for the future work of the zoological institutions. Of course, zoos were not the only target for this campaign: universities of high repute were included too.

Chapter 3

Avril opened the bottle with a corkscrew.

She loved the ritual. Wine bottles with real corks had died out over a hundred years ago. Some wine buffs still had corks, which they traded like pieces of gold. Most wine bottles – when you could get them at all – had metal screw caps. But the vintage wines, which would cost upwards of the equivalent of a month's wage per bottle, had synthetic cork. To be honest you'd have to be an expert to tell the difference. There were no synthetic corks in people's bank deposit boxes. But there were real ones!

There was also a vibrant black market in corks. Some disadvantaged souls, who had had their chips de-activated, sought a trade in corks! It could still be found as a natural resource in a few places on the planet - and there were a few people who could still build and sail an old fashioned sailing boat who would be prepared to risk life and limb to fetch them – for a price. But generally, risking life and limb was passé… After all why would you?

Avril poured the wine carefully into a classically styled crystal glass. She was something of a connoisseur. She held the glass to her nose, closing her eyes so as to concentrate fully on the smoky bouquet. She swung her head slightly from side to side, as if to clear the wandering strand of her long hair from her face. Then she sat down to read. Later she might watch a movie - but what she would not be doing was watching the news.

News reporting had died out fifty years before. There was no longer any point. In the late 21st century it was realised that putting reporters into dangerous environments so that they could get first hand reports of disasters or wars was a bit dangerous. And the law-suits had proved crippling to the news corporations.

At the same time the advance in the quality of artificially generated graphics, and the ease of generating them, meant that you could simulate a disaster or war scene from the editing studio without having to put anyone in the field.

If you really needed local info you would send a drone and then use its copy as the germ for your final news piece. It was a small step from this very ingenious approach to safe reporting, to the generation of completely false news reports.

It didn't happen overnight of course. Someone would have noticed! No, it happened bit by bit: a scene here, a bulletin there, until gradually the viewing stats dwindled. Advertiser income dropped and people realised that they were quite happy not knowing what was happening around the planet. No, Avril would not be watching the news, she had no interest in such things. And she had no interest whatsoever in the previous occupant of her bright, shiny, rose-tinted apartment!

Gerry had had a confusing day.

Everything had started as normal but by lunch time he had realised he had a new existence. Only a trained observer would have noticed his reaction to discovering that he had lost his freedom. He stood still for some minutes, as if he had suddenly forgotten where he was going.

His right hand found its way to his forehead, the middle finger tracing the line of his eyebrow. His eyes seemed focused on the middle distance where the images of his imagined scenarios seemed to be located.

He had known a few other people who had been selected in this way. The trouble was that you only hear rumours about what happens. You can spend every day working alongside someone and you might or might not suspect that they have some special attribute that might attract attention. But when, on the next day, they fail to turn up you don't get a chance to ask them any useful questions. Along with various other privileges, your access to video-coms would be cut off. So the daily or weekly sessions you might have had with a friend of relative ceased.

Most rumours came from outside society – from *deacts*. And who would trust what they had to say! However, in the absence of any other information, you would naturally mull over what they told you.

The best picture that Gerry had been able to construct was that there were some individuals who possessed special talents and demonstrated a particularly successful work track record, and who were therefore required by the Hub to do special work. In a way it was rather romantic. Who wouldn't want to be special! But there was something a bit sinister about it. Rather like being chosen to be a human sacrifice in an ancient Aztec civilisation – thought Gerry. Anyway, whatever this mysterious path had held for other people, now held out the same future for Gerry. He savoured a mixture of fear and excitement. Actually, not much fear. After all, the system – the Hub - had treated him very well so far. Everything he needed was provided. He had comfort, food and shelter, and access to any form of recreation he might ever imagine. So why would he imagine that his new life would be any different.

His naïve confidence was entirely well placed. In a way. He raised his eyebrows briefly, as if discarding an unfruitful chain of thought. The only thing on his mind now was the fact that he had no partner. He had had a few relationships in the past and they had been ok – maybe a bit confusing; he had never really come to terms with his emotions. But he had never thought that there was any urgency about it. Now that he was coming to terms to being 'selected' it was dawning on him that there would be far less chance of finding a partner than before.

Well, that was what he supposed. After all, in reality he had no notion of what being selected would mean. He had never spoken to anyone who had been selected – after the event. They simply disappeared. For all he knew they might be dead! Now that he was chosen, and was clearly alive, he had reason to hope that the

18

others he had known would still be alive too. He might, perhaps, even meet them!

Meanwhile, that primitive mating urge was generating all sorts of unwelcome thoughts in his brain. Strange, he thought, that these were the dominant thoughts. So far as he could tell he had lost his apartment, lost his use of a car, didn't know where he was going to spend the night or eat – yet all he could worry about was being alone. Or maybe it was not so surprising.

Anyway, worrying about it was not going to provide him with supper or a bed. So, at the end of the day, he signed off from his lab-book on his interactive tablet and went to try the doors. This time one of the internal doors from the main corridor opened for him.

He had never had access to this section of the building before and he began to find the new experience quite pleasurable. The corridor led past different offices and what appeared to be entrances to some of the animal enclosures. He had seen them all before – but from the other side. Now he was behind the scenes. He felt a sense of privilege.

Nevertheless he resisted the temptation to try each door. He certainly didn't expect to be spending the night in an animal enclosure! At the end of the corridor the door opened and the soothing voice welcomed him;

"Good evening Gerry. Welcome to your new home."

Gerry opened the door tentatively. Inside he found an apartment of some luxury. The rooms were considerably larger than those of his last apartment. There was more furniture. There was a drinks cabinet – a great luxury. Around the main room there were six more doors. Five of them were perfectly normal in size and scale. He tried them in turn.

One led to a vast kitchen – and on the table a welcome card and a bottle of wine! He interrupted his tour of the new premises to pour himself a glass. Another led to the bathroom, with

19

sumptuous fittings and stylish lighting. The next three led to bedrooms, of equal size, but differing and distinct furnishings. Three of his favourite periods of décor in fact!

The sixth door was like a wall of doors – like the hinged room dividers that people used to have… but it would not open. The smooth voice announced;

"Sorry Gerry – this door is not accessible at this time."

"When will it be?" he asked.

"Access is programmed for 9.30 am Gerry. Please be ready."

Gerry stood open mouthed, staring at the door. He wasn't surprised about the programmed timing. That was part and parcel of his life. But, please be ready? – ready for what? He tried another question.

"What happens at 9.30?"

"Access is programmed for 9.30 am Gerry. Please be ready."

He tried a few more times, rephrasing the question but each time he only got the same answer. He shrugged his shoulders and turned his attention to the wine glass. For all his life he had been controlled by automatic doors and vehicles and everything had always turned out alright. Why should he be worried now? In a way he was quite excited about what would happen at 9.30.

Chapter 4

Avril finished her wine and the movie at about the same time. It was a little before her normal bed time but she had had a tiring day, with all the excitement of moving house. She put in a video call to her mother in Alexandria.

"Darling! How are you? How was your move?"

Avril's mother spoke like a machine gun – words just kept on coming. It didn't seem to matter whether you listened or responded or just kept silent. As long as she could see your face she kept on talking. After half an hour of it Avril's face was beginning to show the stress she was feeling inside.

"Mother! – listen."

She knew the rather formal name would catch her attention.

"Darling – have I done something wrong?"

"No more than usual. I called to talk to you, to let you know about my new apartment."

"Oh yes – how is it, do you like it? Is it like your old one? – better I expect..."

"It's fine, yes it's better, bigger and I think I shall be happy here. Bye."

With that she ended the conversation. She had long learnt that one had to be brutal – if you wanted a life of your own. She was reflecting on the fact that the next day she had to prepare some papers relating to the acquisition of another small library by the World Genetic Bank. Compulsory acquisitions were comparatively simple because there was no legal process of appeal. If the WGB decided they needed your institution they had statutory powers to acquire it. In practical terms it made very little difference to the running of the place and sometimes Avril wondered why they bothered with the process at all. But the main impact was technical. WGB would henceforth have the right to access the institution's data and research libraries.

The minute after her documentation was complete it would be transferred to the Court which would automatically process it and issue the order. Within minutes technical operatives would descend upon the institution and their PIDACs would have full access to the technical resources of the institution. By the early hours of the next morning the institution would be an homogenous part of WGB and no one would think twice about it.

Occasionally Avril wondered about the legitimacy of her work. She took a high moral stance and would not engage in any kind of activity unless she had satisfied herself of its legitimacy. Hence her career in law. When she had started in the WGB acquisitions department she had been satisfied that there were all the correct checks and balances in place but, over time, she began to wonder whether some essential human rights weren't being obscured. But for the most part she was happy that she was involved in a scientific programme that would work for the benefit of mankind in general. And she was quite happy with her remuneration in particular!

After her shower and ablutions she settled down in her new bed and kissed two fingers before placing them gently on the picture of her mother. Her mother was everything to her. Mothers generally were everything to their offspring. Fathers, on the other hand, barely existed.

Chapter 5

Gerry's work at the zoo had included, amongst other things, comparing the effects of natural reproduction – in which a male and a female of the species mated physically, with what his species now practised. It went by the name of 'replication'. Sperm cells were collected clinically and analysed for their genetic content. Those which matched the replication requirement were then harvested and banked. A similar process applied to female ova. When a woman was detailed to replicate, by the Hub, she would draw up a specification of the ovum-sperm set and the Hub would find the closest match.

In this strange, dry scientific utopia, it was still felt to be ethically important that parents had a choice in the way their offspring were created. The replication lab would marry the constituent parts and the would-be mother would be called in at the appropriate time for the implant. A message would be sent to the chosen father, which would appear on his information board, advising him that a contract had been entered into. He would automatically receive a data-stream of information about his descendant but he would only even meet him or her if the mother so desired. When the system had first been introduced, fathers spent long hours and small fortunes trying to get to see their offspring. But they soon tired of it.

This left both males and females free to meet and form emotional relationships without the burden of responsibility. Generally both genders preferred the freedom that emanated from that arrangement to the old fashioned and messy arrangement! For that reason Avril's mother meant everything to her. Her father was little more than an interesting irrelevance.

Next morning Gerry was up at 7 a.m. as usual. He had a light breakfast and read some professional journals on his tablet. He reflected on how strange it seemed to still be using this ancient technology, when 3D retinal projection enabled a whole universe of experience and data to be injected straight into his visual field. But there was something tactile about a tablet that you didn't get with a hologram.

As usual he was reading about genetics and historical variants. Classification of human DNA, along with research into the contents of asteroids and some of the solar system planets, had led to interesting discoveries about the origins of life of earth. Whilst most life forms seemed to have their origin firmly planted on planet earth, there were some DNA sections that seemed to be quite alien. Interestingly they matched up with primitive bacteria-like life-forms evident in asteroid material and even found on some of the planets other than earth. Because the 'foreign' sections were so foreign, they were only evident in a very few examples of creatures on earth - and even more rare in human DNA. The article Gerry was reading described research into this rare human variety.

WGB had commented, as a rider to the article, that the isolation and preservation of example of the species with this particular section of DNA had been made the top priority of the WGB and all institutions would be tasked accordingly. "Great!" thought Gerry. "WGB comes up with a really interesting programme and I'm isolated in a zoo!" He was still musing on this when the smooth synthetic voice made an announcement.

"Sorry Gerry but door F will not be opening today. We apologise for any inconvenience."

Gerry chuckled to himself. Since he had neither any idea what lay behind door F, nor any desire therefore to open it, he would not be inconvenienced in the slightest by its reluctance to open! He took a protein drink from the cooler and left his new apartment to go to work.

Chapter 6

Avril also left her new home and let her car drive her to the office. Her somewhat placid nature allowed her to be driven by a machine without any sense of discomfort. Her motto was *que sera sera*. Big decisions she would take ages to ponder. But the routine ones she was happy to leave to fate, other people or well-designed machines.

Sometimes she would work at home. But employers found that human interaction still motivated people in ways that could not be replicated by technology. As she entered her office her superior, Melody, passed her a file. This was not a physical entity of course. Passing a file meant initiating a mutual perception session (MPS), in which two or more people's 3D Holoviewer would project the same virtual scene onto each person's retina. The Holoviewer was also old technology. It looked like a pair of glasses, but it contained a stereo projector that delivered images straight onto the retina. The result was a stunning 3d image appearing in front of your eyes. In this scenario you could visualise files and objects and pass them around. Behind the scenes the Hub would create the appropriate access protocols so that the recipient now had exclusive access to the data contained in the file. The file related to the Smithsonian Zoo, already acquired by WGB some years ago - and it was a day late being processed. Consequently Melody was not in the best of moods.

However, the content of this particular file was not concerned with the acquisition of institutions. It referred to a particular object, a member of one of the species preserved and protected by that zoo. The initial acquisition had been processed the day before but the process needed a final authorisation before the exhibit could be put on display. The species was Hs53. The instance was referred to by a unique ID. It was a 24 digit number, the significance of which was completely unknown to Avril. It was also completely unknown to its owner.

Chapter 7

By a complete fluke of chance, Avril and Gerry were both thinking about the same thing that morning. Species Hs53. Avril had only the vaguest understanding of what the term referred to. She knew it was a reference to an animal species but more than that she neither knew nor cared to know.

On the other hand, Gerry knew more about Species Hs53 than any sane person would ever want to know. And he was very excited, because the rare DNA section that WGB had just made its top priority, was uniquely found in Hs53. What Avril knew that Gerry didn't know, was the actual identity of one of the only four known examples of an Hs53 currently in captivity. She knew it by the name "operative 36U1HJ83K7GYR485VQL10964". She wondered what it looked like. She wondered just what it was! And she wondered what all the fuss was about. Her role was normally associated with acquisition of property and information. Not animals. They normally came with the institution; and if an institution wanted to acquire a new sample it would simply issue a requisition. There was no legal process apart from that simple 'document'. However in this case the acquisition of a sample of a species had landed on her desk.

Deftly and quickly she accessed the legal database and searched for statutes and other legal instruments that were relevant. After several minutes of searching, she discovered something that made the hairs on the back of neck stand on end. Species Hs53 was a form not just of another animal. It was of a *human*. No wonder it could not be processed the ordinary way. It was not unprecedented for human samples to be requisitioned; but usually they were drawn from the de-activated pool – from the *deacts*. Admittedly this was rather a messy process, since de-activated persons were outside the System altogether.

However, their PIDACs would still transmit their ID and whereabouts, so the System could at least know where they were. Recovering them was a job for the police.

They tended to rather enjoy it. It was a bit like hunting. The Hub gave you their coordinates to the nearest 5m or so. But there was a huge adrenaline rush as you took your patrol vehicle outside your normal area into no-man's land. Some of the deacts were armed – with sticks or stones mainly. So there was a fair chance that you might get hurt. This was where the skill came in – making sure that you took them by surprise, before they could aim a shot at you. According to the protocol you were meant to stun them remotely; but where's the fun in that! Most officers preferred to have a bit of hand-to-hand and would mark up their trophy count in the office. Officially, of course, it was frowned on – it put you at risk.

However, this sample of Hs53 was not a deact. That made it altogether different. The request was for a warrant to reduce the individual's rights from that of a free person to 'retained'. There were several classes of 'retained' including convicted criminals, socially unacceptable individuals, revolutionaries and so forth. And a category that Avril had not seen before; 'research subject'. Avril looked up the protocol, checked that the appropriate processes and risk assessment had been carried out and formulated the requisition. She pressed the button and shrugged her shoulders. The new category may have scared her a little but the process was properly defined, so there was no reason to worry. *Que sera sera…*

She made herself a cup of coffee.

Chapter 8

The soothing synthetic voice disturbed Gerry's thoughts. He had been making notes on one of the samples that he was studying when the voice started.

"Access to door F is now authorised. Gerry, please go through."

Curious, but not alarmed, Gerry left his tablet on the table and went over to the vast multiple panelled door. Unseen and unheard his PIDAC communicated with the door control and it folded back almost silently. What Gerry saw before his eyes shocked him. It was completely unfamiliar and he simply couldn't make any sense of it. His face revealed more emotion than had been seen in him for more than a decade.

Chapter 9

For forty five years now Zurich had been the headquarters of the International Intelligence Corporation. It had originally been a comparatively small IT company specialising in Artificial Intelligence software but, after the collapse of the World Wide Web, it had picked up the pieces and created a new web out of the ashes of the old.

The old system had become vulnerable to cyber-attacks by terrorist groups. When the major western governments decided to act in consort, they chose Switzerland as the location most suited to guard the digital assets of the world. It was a shrewd move. After all, the Swiss had some considerable experience in looking after the world's wealth and financial secrets. Why not entrust the digital infrastructure of society to them as well?

The CEO of IIC at the time happened to be related to a senior government official and his company's proposal for a self-organising system to manage the world's information structure impressed the right people.

Although no one seriously believed that AI systems had anything resembling consciousness, their ability to solve complex problems, and in particular recognise new potential threats from cyber-attacks, was now vastly superior to anything humans could manage. Thus the Hub of this new 'web' was located deep in a rock fortress somewhere near Zurich, with repeater hubs distributed across the planet.

"In a way, the world is becoming a massive super-brain."

Carl Fische, the senior analyst at ICC, was lecturing the new intake on the growth of this information network. Carl was tall, about 6' 2", well-built, though not seemingly fat. He was in his fifties and clearly at the top of his game. His hair was retreating and turning a silver grey. He oozed confidence and responded to any kind of attack with a big beefy grin that seemed to say 'You can try if you like!' A hand went up at the front of the class.

29

"Professor Fische, isn't our reliance on this technology potentially dehumanising?"

There was always one person among the fresh new graduates who felt uncomfortable about assigning responsibility for decision making to machines. Carl put his head slightly to one side and closed one eye – a sure sign that he was concentrating.

"Well, you could see it that way. Personally I see it as all part of the process of evolution. I mean, when the first fish-like creature abandoned the security of the sea and started to evolve into a land-living variant, you could see that as a negative – giving up its natural home. Or the first step in a process that led eventually to the development of humans." He finished with a chuckle.

"Do you mean that eventually machines will replace humans?"

"Oh I doubt that. But they will and already have developed as a result of evolutionary, competitive processes and as they evolve, we will evolve too."

"Are you sure that humans can keep up? Won't they just become an inferior species and be dominated?"

He stepped forward slightly as if entering their secret space.

"Look, I see it more as a process of symbiosis. Two species that need each other."

Carl spoke with a twinkle in his eye. He had worked with the Hub for several decades now and saw no reason to fear the rise of machine life. Whilst it was true that the Hub controlled increasingly large areas of human activity – from power stations to surveillance systems, the food supply chain to university research projects – its activity was founded on the Prime Directives. And they could not be tinkered with by the Hub itself.

Actually it is not entirely accurate to say the Hub controlled all this. The Hub was more of an abstract concept really. There were many hubs like the one in Zurich, distributed all over the world.

This provided redundancy, so that an attack on a number of hubs could not destroy the whole system. However, the Zurich hub had precedence over the rest. At least at the moment. In the unlikely event of the Zurich hub being disabled, then ultimate authority would pass to one of the other hubs, following a protocol agreed by the International Directorate for Information Control, IDIC.

So when people talked about the Hub, what they usually meant was the control system within this distributed network. Most people could master that concept. And it was this Hub, implementing the Prime Directives, processing information on a gargantuan scale, from billions of sources across the planet, that had decided that operative 36U1HJ83K7GYR485VQL10964 should be demoted to 'retained' status and become a research subject. The reason? Quite simply that operative 36U1HJ83K7GYR485VQL10964 had been discovered to be an example of Hs53; and Hs53 contained in its DNA a remnant of a prehistoric hominoid that had been extinct long before modern man had even learned to talk. Prime Directive 247 was there to protect any such remnants for posterity and research. That was the reason that Gerry could no longer leave the zoo, use his car or live in his old apartment.

Of course nobody told him. There was no need for him to be informed. Operatives of 'research subject' status had no rights to such information. Avril knew this – she had checked the protocols.

Gerry found himself staring. The door, or doors, had opened, folding back silently like a room divider. But they did not reveal a room. There was merely a small strip of carpet in front of him and then a wall. Not a normal wall, but a transparent one, apparently made of glass: from floor to ceiling and extending the full width of the room. His eyes were fixed on what was on the other side of the wall. The view was not unfamiliar to Gerry. He had passed by many times, though not paying much attention.

Immediately outside the wall was a walkway and on the other side of that another glass wall. This was the view he was used to. Only the previous day he had walked along the same walkway and looked into the enclosure which now faced him. In it was one of the zoo's exhibits, a sample of a rare chimp species found in the Amazonian rain forest.

Gerry's first reaction, when finally he did react, was to assume that there had been a mistake. A glitch in the system. He started blinking at last – his eyes moving around the images being created by his analytical imagination. Then he focussed on the scene before him. He wasn't phased or upset. This was merely another logical puzzle to unravel.

As an undergraduate he had always enjoyed logical exercises. Unlike other students, who enjoyed setting them and watching as people suffered the frustration of not being able to solve them, Gerry enjoyed cracking them. And he was quick.

He examined the glass wall from edge to edge to see if there was a release or catch. He knew he wouldn't find one. This was a high security enclosure. Such designs were used not only for potentially dangerous exhibits but also for relatively benign but very intelligent ones – like the chimp facing him now. They had such dexterity and strength that they could dismantle most structures with ease, given time. And time is one commodity that is not in short supply if you're an exhibit!

The chimp stopped in the middle of stripping some bark from a twig in order to cast a glance at the new arrival. It continued chewing. The new arrival wasn't that interesting. In fact Gerry paid far more attention to the chimp than it did to him but then, that was his job. He knew there was no point in shouting for help – these units were sound-proofed so that visitors and researchers weren't constantly distracted by the noises their occupants made. Instead he returned to the apartment and checked every room and every door.

He could still access the corridor that led to the apartment. But none of the doors leading off it would grant him access. The soft and comforting voice that had given him helpful information or instructions for all of his life, until now, was silent. Doors either opened or didn't. In the kitchen there was a food store which was re-stocked via a small hatch at the back. Gerry knew that behind the hatch there was a security air lock. There would be no way of getting out through that. In any case, even if he were to manage it, it would only lead to the service network. This comprised a system of tunnels about 30 cm square. It was populated only by a set of specially designed operatives.

Operatives, in Gerry's world, were any kind of asset that performed actions. That could include people. But also machines. Some were wheeled – designed for working in spaces that had a smooth floor and no stairs. Interestingly this did not include cars, since cars did not have any form of autonomy. They just obeyed instructions. Operatives, on the other hand, all possessed some element of autonomy, which enabled the intelligence of the 'Hub' to be distributed amongst billions of machines. Military vehicles, however, were operatives because they did have autonomy. This enabled a fighting force to develop its own strategy and tactics on the ground, even when communication with the Hub was cut off. Non-military vehicles did not have autonomy. This was deliberate. In the past, terrorist and other banned groups would make use of non-military vehicles for their campaigns. By deliberately 'crippling' non-military vehicles, such unauthorised groups would always be at a tactical disadvantage.

The operatives that inhabited the service network behind this hatch were wheeled. They only ever operated on a level surface. On the other hand, the operative that had just entered Gerry's apartment to clean it waddled about on three legs.

Three legs are more stable than two. Human beings could never have evolved three legs because of their inherited skeletal structure. Evolution would have had to have taken a very different direction billions of years before humanity arrived to enable that development. However, artificial operatives can be designed from scratch. Like with wheels, or tripod limbs. Gerry was not surprised to see the tripod operative. He had seen them daily all his working life. In fact he barely noticed it. Except for a fleeting consideration of how he might be able to use it to get out of his apartment... but no, that wouldn't work – these operatives also entered and left via a security air lock. Sensors in the secure space would detect Gerry's presence – the PIDAC would alert them. And since these air locks were designed to prevent living animals escaping they really were air locks. Ultimately the Hub could evacuate it and any living organism within it would die.

There was no chance of holding the operative hostage in any way, either, since one of the Prime Directives ensured that machine operatives would defend themselves only up to the point when doing so would compromise security. This was basic to the whole Hub system. On a larger scale, each hub would defend itself too. One Prime Directive – PD 139 - covered the necessity of self-preservation. The over-arching purpose of the Prime Directives was to protect human life and to preserve what remained of the diversity of life on the planet.

Therefore each hub had a duty to defend itself so that it could perform its primary function of supporting and defending humanity. But if the hub were in a situation where its own existence threatened that underlying duty – for example if it were to be captured by a terrorist group – then its duty was to self-destruct. That way control would be assumed by another hub which was not being compromised. So, trying to use this tripod operative as a means of escape would be doomed to failure. It would self-destruct in the security air lock.

Gerry's mind had been racing for several minutes now. He had tried to keep calm but the increasing sense of fear was generating high adrenalin levels, which in turn were making his brain work harder and faster. Compared with his normal academic routine, where experiments and research tasks were meticulously planned and carefully executed, now for once he was thinking on his feet - and he was rather enjoying the experience.

However, another part of his brain was already anticipating everything he was thinking of. He had an intimate knowledge of the protocols that determined security in the zoo. All human operatives there had to − it was part of their health and safety routine; and he knew that every security feature had been designed rigorously and tested against the most ingenious creatures.

However, there was one glimmer of hope. Until now, zoo enclosures had only ever been designed for non-human exhibits. They hadn't been designed to cope with human intelligence. This glimmer was somewhat mollified by Gerry's recollection that the systems were controlled by the Hub, which already had algorithms and strategies developed by artificial intelligence that far outstripped human intelligence. Moreover they were reactive and predictive. If he were to come up with some feasible strategy, as soon as he tried to implement it a billion computational units, distributed throughout the Hub, would be analysing his actions and predicting his next move. He began to feel like a small child trying to play chess against a grand master.

Gradually the adrenalin dissipated and Gerry came down from his unfamiliar high. He began to suspect that he was up against a logical puzzle that even he might not be able to solve. Like many caged animals before him, he assumed a foetal position in the corner of the room.

Chapter 10

While Gerry was considering his future, Avril was working on the next of a dozen or so legal documents. Although most decisions were made automatically, they still required oversight. The court, for example, that had endorsed Gerry's status demotion was a virtual one; there were no judge or jury, and the Hub produced and weighed arguments in an AI environment. However, its arguments and verdict had to be open to scrutiny and certain levels of decision were mandatorily endorsed by a human expert. This was Avril's role.

She had been in the post five years and so far had never had cause to challenge a single decision of the court. She didn't expect ever to have to. She wasn't alone. There were a dozen or so co-workers in the office. They would meet formally once a week to review the cases they had overseen and sometimes would hold off endorsing a verdict until they had had a case meeting.

Alternatively, if they had a pressing question and the court required a speedy endorsement, they could have an informal conversation with a colleague. Technically the conversations were informal – they were not minuted and, if there was an appeal, their informal conversation would not be admitted as evidence.

However, just about every conversation inside the office was recorded and stored away somewhere, and the content of the conversation would be analysed by the Hub. The resulting opinion would be attached to the person's work record and would be used in assessing career moves. Everyone knew this and consequently everyone was careful.

It wasn't a 'Big Brother' thing. You didn't feel that you were constantly being observed, as it had happened since before you were born. It was natural. Though if you wanted a real conversation you knew you had to go off grid – a surprisingly difficult thing to do. There may not be voice recorders in the street but there were video cameras - and the Hub had sophisticated lip-reading algorithms.

In the early days protest groups had gone wild about these invasions of privacy but a few suitably aggressive and well targeted terrorist attacks soon convinced people that they were better off in a world where everyone was observed than in one where they weren't. A few degrees of freedom weren't worth making a fuss about. The problem also became auto-remedial. Those individuals and groups who resolutely and defiantly objected to such developments tended to get involved in anti-social behaviour, leading ultimately to being de-activated. No one really cared what happened to them – their problems were self-inflicted after all.

Avril wasn't any different from the rest. The Hub had quickly learnt that the best way to protect the human species from itself was to ensure that people were very well catered for and comfortable. That tended to diminish unrest and aggression, and all the studies had shown that the negative effects of war and terrorism had vastly outweighed the sum of all other negative impact of human activity. Aggression and overpopulation – they were the two most dangerous by-products of the immense success of the human species. Now that population growth was controlled by the Hub, at least in the West, the demands of the population could be matched with the availability of resources.

The only elements that were outside the Hub's benign control were the deacts and the unknown number of people who lived in the 'uncivilised' world – the East. The first, you grew up ignoring in the street and they tended to take themselves off for termination after a while. The latter you just didn't know about – how could you?

Max Brunner, however, did know about them. He and a select few other top ranking officials of IDIC knew all about them.

37

Max was medium height, quite stocky with black hair cut short. He always dressed impeccably and was a master of the big picture. His face revealed little except what would appear to be an ideal poker player. He did everything deliberately. If he was quiet or listening he would do it with a hundred percent attention. If he was talking it would be with speed and precision. If he asked a question it would be pointed and intelligent. He always seemed to do very little but achieved a great deal. People loved to have him about.

The executive members of IDIC were unofficially appointed by a rather shadowy group of trustees known as the Zurich group. They had inherited the mantle of the now defunct Bilderberg group. Their purpose had changed over the years, to become the oversight of human development across the world, though with a membership largely drawn from the Western nations, the needs of the more populous East were somewhat subordinate.

Max Brunner, being both the leader of IDIC and the de facto leader of the Zurich group, had a level of power and authority which would be the envy of many world leaders, had they known.

There was no constitution, no minutes were kept, ostensibly no decisions were made, but the group gained its power from the influence of its members: government leaders, past leaders, well behaved dictators, leaders of large religious groups, eminent scientists, owners of large multi-nationals and a number of extremely wealthy individuals. By no means all members of these groups were present. Only the chosen few and it was just a few. Membership was by invitation only. They all had a common interest in the survival of the planet and would communicate secretly about national and internal politics.

To ensure this could happen, they created a secure communication channel – Vector - which used a virtually unbreakable synchronous encryption algorithm. Even the Hub, with all its massed billions of intelligent processors, from the chip embedded in your fridge, to a vast array of servers dedicated to weather prediction, even it could not access the channel. It never would – its secrecy was one of the Prime Directives. Anyone coming remotely near to even talking about it would be deactivated.

It was the Zurich group who masterminded the adoption of the Prime Directives and appointed the IDIC. A small team within IDIC would gather information about the East and report back to the trustees. Max and his team had been worrying for some years about the impact of the East on the global picture.

The East comprised countries or nations that were outside the grasp of the Hub. Some were go-it-alone independents who suspected the motives of the West. Others had a political history of aggression or denial of human rights. Or others again were just anti-social. Countries were treated by the Zurich group in much the same way as individuals were treated by the Hub.

In the early 21st century the world population had been around six billion. Now the West numbered only two billion. However, the East contained an unknown number of humans – probably more than six billion by itself. This represented a double threat. First there was always the possibility that they might develop a unified coalition and become a tangible enemy. Second, and more likely and more insidious, they might threaten the very resources upon which the West depended for its existence.

The Hub had a special subset of activity devoted to modelling and trying to predict the behaviour of these nations. But without all the detailed and wide ranging data that it could gain from the West, its predictions for the East were very primitive: about as accurate as forecasting the weather! This was the Achilles heel in the Zurich machine. And Max was concerned. The Zurich group were concerned too. They had been for a decade or more. If the truth were to be told, they had probably been concerned at some level since they were young men. For this reason Max had been tasked with the job of getting the subset of the Hub responsible for modelling the East to run some feasibility models.

A number of them were based on attempting to replicate in the East political and academic developments that were part of the West's history. Not that anyone had much faith that that would work. Surely they would have come on board already. Other models were more radical. It had been decided five years previously that the Hub should be adapted to be able to implement any one of the models. In order to maintain secrecy, the models were merely numbered, one through five. Model five presented the most radical solution.

Chapter 11

Max got off the plane and walked across the tarmac to the waiting car. As he got into the car he took off his very dark sun glasses and put them away in his inside pocket. The breast pocket of his jacket was reserved for his pocket handkerchief. Today it was red with white spots.

The car was empty and as soon as he got in an official came up and handed him the key. This was not a regular vehicle. It was old fashioned. It had a steering wheel. It needed a driver. It was not connected to the Hub. It had a key to turn it on. It was, however, an electric vehicle. The only carbon fuelled vehicles left were those in museums – or of course in countries in the East. All the senior executives of IDIC and all the members of the Zurich group had the right to use an off-grid car. They had no tracking devices, no eavesdropping facilities. They were entirely private.

Zuricor – the Swiss independent company charged with protecting the members of the Zurich group and the high level members of IDIC – was there to ensure these standards were maintained. Max drove through the VIP gate at the aero-terminal and sped his way to the 'Castle'. His driving was just like his approach to every other part of his life, measured and efficient. One of his hobbies was racing ancient cars so he knew exactly how far he could push the vehicle.

Glanzenberg Castle had been a castle ruin and still was to all intents and purposes. It was a site of enormous historical interest and value and, like many very valuable sites, had been closed to the public for the best part of a century. Whilst on the surface it hadn't changed for centuries, below ground there had been built a formidable bunker. It had a number of rooms, its own power supply, air cleaning system and direct, though anonymous, access to the Hub. In order for the Zurich group members' identities to be preserved it was essential that no record of the group ever existed in the Hub's memory.

But, like the old fashioned car that Max was driving, the Castle was 'clean' – you could talk freely. Max and a select few members of the Zurich group and ICAD would be meeting there later, accompanied by Carl Fische.

There was, as usual, no formal agenda, but they all knew why they would be there. They arrived punctually before 4 pm. A team of human operatives had been drafted in to provide tea and cakes. Some customs never seemed to change. The room was sparsely furnished. This made it easier for Zuricor operatives to check it for bugs. The girls wore traditional long red skirts, red headscarves and had tightly laced vests, accentuating their shape. Traditional Swiss dress – once. But for the topic of conversation, the scene could have been set two hundred years in the past.

Max was first of the VIPs to arrive, closely followed by Carl. Carl chatted happily with the girls, not quite flirting but almost. They warmed to his charm and possibly to his white beard. The chair of the Zurich group followed. He was the Prime Minister of France, Jacques Barre. His role was elected annually, though in practice it was the leader of the group who controlled the chairmanship. By politics he was right wing. In fact all the members of the Zurich group were right wing. And they were all male.

The United States currently had a socialist administration, so its President – who otherwise might well have been invited – was not present. There was, however, a prominent US industrialist in the room, Eddie Wilson. He had forebears in the powerful oil empire. Oil, of course, had ceased to be a profitable commodity some decades previously, since the rise of the use of hydrogen.

Comparatively recent developments in carbon fibre technology had overcome the longstanding obstacle to using pure hydrogen – its very small molecule size. This had prevented the mass transportation of the gas on an industrial scale, and development of new technology had been thwarted by the ignorance and defensive policies of the oil industry.

Eddie Wilson had been the first of his very conservative family to jump ship and invest heavily in hydrogen. He had previously made speculative purchases of land in uninhabited desert coastal regions – ideal for the production of electricity from sun light, and the extraction of hydrogen from sea water by electrolysis. Eddie's far-sightedness, or good luck, was soon rewarded. The rest of his family invested, the technology took off, and he became the wealthiest man in the West. Far-sightedness and commercial success of that quality did not go unnoticed by the Zurich group; they needed him on board!

The four men exchanged confident hand-shakes and sat down to begin their meeting. From the body language one would assume that Carl was the dominant character – tall and extrovert. Max appeared reticent and studious but you could tell that he was being covertly observed by all the other three. When he spoke everyone else would shut up.

Carl was first to address them all. He had called the meeting, so it was literally his shout. He stood in the middle of the room, with no desk in front to provide psychological defence. His broad palms were spread facing the rest of the group. He was in his element.

"Gentlemen, as you know, we have been concerned for some time about the security of the future of the West." Within that one short sentence he dropped his smile and eyed every member of his audience with an expression that said *Look, I'm levelling with you.*

"From our current research we estimate that the population of the East is increasing by about 13% per annum. Its carbon footprint is increasing by 15% per annum. And the outbreaks of civil aggression are on the up as well. We have been modelling five scenarios that might help to turn these numbers around but so far none of them has shown any sign of working. Models one to four we have trialled in various small countries - but with no significant effect. Model five, of course, cannot realistically be trialled."

No one ever considered it would need to be. It was there as a place holder – something to consider theoretically if none of the other models showed any promise.

"The problem is that according to our predictions from the Hub, the situation could go critical within the next twelve months."

Everyone had a pretty good idea of what 'going critical' meant. Geographically, the East was isolated by expanses of ocean, ranges of mountains and vast lengths of border markers. The border markers were electrified but also protected from above by drone-born lasers. Much of the border was also heavily irradiated by the effects of previous nuclear exchanges.

Incursions were few. The West, of course, knew nothing of the incursions – there was no news. The East, relying on scrappy and out of date technology, heard rumours and elaborated on them. Since they never heard stories of heroes crossing the border and returning wealthy, or even returning at all, they generally behaved on the basis that the borders were best left alone. However, the four people in the castle bunker knew that when you put a lot of deprived humans together there is the danger of mass uprisings and large scale heroic action. Many of the border defences worked mainly by fear. And when there is an uprising, fear retreats. The situation goes critical.

There was also the issue of trade. The West still depended on the East for cheap resources, though it had made great strides towards independence. The one resource that was really vulnerable was hydrogen. Whilst it was still true that most of the gas fields were in unpopulated regions of desert, they were mostly very near, or even on the wrong side of, the border. In extremis they could not really be defended.

For the East to go critical, therefore, was unthinkable.

"Look, I don't like the look of this at all."

Edwin was launching into an emotional contribution.

"I have a lot at stake here – so does the whole of my family."

"I think, Mr Wilson, that the whole world has a lot at stake."

Max's words were calm and measured. He was used to containing the geyser of wrath that swelled in him whenever Ed spoke. Of course, Ed had to be there, though everyone wished he weren't. It wasn't a political disagreement. Max was probably as far to the right as one could get. He just couldn't stand the fact that Ed couldn't see the big picture.

"The thing is, Ed, it's not anything that we can do anything about. Not directly. As you know, all our systems and policies are controlled by the Hub. It has more knowledge than we can ever comprehend. It has analytical algorithms that we don't even know about – no one does. But it has a superb track record of managing humans and other animals, in a way that we could never emulate."

"Then what's the point of our being here?"

Jacques Barre was clearly irritated that his time was being wasted on some hypothetical world scenario.

"That's why Carl asked us to be here today."

Carl rose to his feet again. His face showed a slight expression of impatience. He cast his gaze left of stage as if he were working hard to contain his feelings. It was, of course, well-practised.

"The Hub succeeds as it does partly because of its enormous effective intelligence, with its processing distributed across so many billions of intelligent devices."

"Including my garden weed-bot?" Max was introducing some humour.

"Yes including those, in a way. They all have a swathe of sensors which feed information into the Hub. In a way it's a bit like an ant colony. Individually ants are pretty dumb. But as a collective they're brilliant. The Hub is similar, but increased in intelligence by a factor of several billion."

"Your weed-bot isn't that clever, on its own. It matches plants against its on-board database and removes those that are flagged as weeds. But where it gets clever is in its cooperation. When it plucks a weed it tells the Hub. When it leaves a plant untouched it tells the Hub. When you stop it from pulling a particular weed because you like it, it tells the Hub. When it finds a plant it doesn't recognise it tells the Hub. The Hub will compare the new plant with any other data it has from other weed-bots, maybe comparing the reaction of their different owners. It matches your gardener profile against other people with similar ones and checks how they react. If they ordered their bots to remove the new plant, your bot will too. Now it's getting really intelligent. And that is just a simple scenario."

"So can we make it more intelligent? Is that the answer?"

"Well, no, actually. I mean, yes we can increase its intellect, as it were, and we are doing, all the time. But that's the wrong question. The foundation of the Hub is the set of Prime Directives that govern its decision making."

He paused, with his hand against his mouth, clearly measuring his words and his audience before making a suggestion that would change the whole future of the Hub and the whole planet.

Chapter 12

Avril's work was somewhat tedious but being naturally unambitious this didn't perturb her. But she did take some satisfaction from knowing that she was acting in a sort of auditing role, making sure that that due legal process was followed. So far she had never had to challenge a document or decision that came across her desk.

But if she had to she knew that there would be a protocol for dealing with the issue. There would initially be a remote MPS, so that she and her boss could access the document and background material. The discussion would of course be on the record. If they both eventually approved the document, it could pass to the next stage. If they differed in their opinion then the issue was escalated to someone at the next level. Generally that would be the last that someone like Avril would know about it. She didn't need to know the outcome, her role was to check, not to adjudicate. She didn't need to learn from experience – the Hub did that. If they both agreed that there was a problem with the document or judgement, it would have to go to an appeal court. This would involve presenting the relevant documentation to a real live judge somewhere. Somewhere could be anywhere. Probably somewhere sunny near the sea.

Avril's work was guided by various protocols. She liked that. It made her feel comfortable. It was detailed but rarely involved matters of any great weight. She was aware, as anyone would be, that behind this vast system of interconnected computers, there was a kind of virtual mind, directing and guiding.

And she was aware also that behind that was a set of guiding principles, the Prime Directives, which kept her and the whole of the West safe and healthy, comfortable and well fed. She had reason to be thankful for those directives. Her whole life had been protected, shaped and, to an extent, inspired by them.

The directives had been put together early on in the life of the Hub and, like many legal structures, it was fashioned out of the wreckage of what had gone before. Loss of human life caused by nuclear power plant disasters; human suffering caused by wars, aggression, terrorism. Aggression fuelled by inequalities between different layers of society. Unstable societies caused by the recklessness of party politics and so called democracies. And the unpredictable vagaries of free market economies. This was the message she had been taught from kindergarten and was happy to believe.

Socialist and communist regimes had failed because people took advantage of nanny state provisions. Capitalist regimes had failed because they were too ruthless or open to corruption by large corporates. The most successful regimes had been benign dictatorships – when you could find them! They tended to provide stable, long term governments with a long view. All these thoughts occasionally swam around Avril's mind. She wondered whether she might have been a politician, in a different age, though she recognised that a lack of ambition would be a serious handicap. But for now, politicians had become a thing of the past. So far as Avril could see, the world was a better place for it!

The Hub, of course, was modelled on the benign dictatorship model. It was a strict society with zero tolerance. If you strayed outside the boundaries of acceptable behaviour you were simply deactivated.

She herself had never suffered this fate of course. But she had been near people who had. One incident occurred when she was relaxing in the park on a Saturday afternoon. There were ducks on the lake. A man was selling ice-creams. She bought one. Various sensors in the ice-cream seller's vehicle would have registered the transaction, and millions of minute, complex relationships in the Hub would have changed slightly. Not that Avril would have noticed. An ice-cream is just an ice-cream. As the seller pressed the transaction button, one of the devices in the van would have communicated with Avril's PIDAC, which in turn would communicate with the accounting system, and her bank account would have debited automatically.

Next to her, on the bench by the lake where she eventually perched to eat her ice cream, there was a younger man. On the face of it there was nothing wrong with him. He was well presented and properly dressed. Not that that mattered especially. However, PIDACs employed GPS technology so that the Hub could monitor which people were getting close or moving away from others.

If someone, because of their behaviour or dress, was constantly met with other people's disapproval, the Hub would know. It could track minute changes in people's behaviour. Although the Hub couldn't smell, it knew from the movements of PIDACs' owners when they smelt something good – or bad. After a week or so of bad reactions, the Hub would politely suggest – in the privacy of your home – that perhaps you needed to attend to your personal hygiene. You weren't going to be deactivated for such a misdemeanor but it might affect your prospects of promotion.

Anyway, this young man wasn't badly dressed and he didn't smell, so far as Avril could tell – and she would know if he did. No, the man decided he had had enough of his ice cream and chucked what was left, in its wrapper, on the floor. The chip in the ice cream wrapper communicated its trajectory to the man's PIDAC, which then calculated that he must have committed a litter offence. The speaker in his ear softly and quietly reminded him about the anti-litter laws. But he was defiant and strode away. The volume of the voice and its nature changed, becoming loud enough for Avril to hear.

"Pick up the litter or be deactivated in twenty seconds."

"Oh fuck you!" the man shouted at the virtual nanny in his ear.

A short beep emanated from the back of the man's neck. Avril knew that this meant the Hub had been as good as its word and that the man was now off the grid. A few minutes later a cleaner operative whizzed along the path and picked up the litter. It ran on little legs – which gave it some mobility around areas with steps and other obstacles. This made the object appear to waddle from side to side, almost as if it were 'tut-tutting'. Avril couldn't help smiling and wondering whether it had learnt that behaviour as a way of disarming more petulant law breakers. Who knew? – the Hub was capable of anything!

As for the man, unless he recanted and went to a civil office for training and reactivation, he would not have anywhere to sleep and wouldn't be able to get anything to eat – not even an ice cream! It was an authoritarian regime. But because there was no human being in the Presidential palace, arbitrarily ordering people about, generally they didn't mind. It was strict and it was fair. And it certainly worked.

Avril's first reaction to this drama unfolding in front of her was shock. But the next weekend, when she saw the man back again, she felt relieved. Clearly he had toed the line and had been reactivated. Apart from the shame, he didn't seem to have suffered in any way. And the park was totally devoid of litter. As to which Prime Directives had been involved in that little drama Avril couldn't really tell. In fact no one could. The neural networks that implemented the Prime Directives and compared them with behaviour patterns were opaque to all humans. A positive consequence of that fact was that it was practicably impossible to fiddle with the system. If you tried you would never be able to predict the outcome.

Chapter 13

It was early evening and Gerry had spent most of the afternoon huddled up on the floor. Partly this was a genuine reaction to the shock of his new situation. Partly it was strategic. He knew that as a research subject and an exhibit, the Hub would be monitoring him closely. Not out of suspicion, but merely because that was what you do with exhibits. You monitor them, learn from them.

But of course the Hub would also be considering security. If Gerry was compliant and biddable, there would be no cause for concern. If he started shouting or hitting the doors and window the Hub would react to this potentially unsociable behaviour and deduce that there was a risk of him trying to escape, thereby risking hurting himself.

Since captives and some exhibits were potentially dangerous, they naturally invoked the Prime Directive ensuring the protection of humans – ordinary, free human beings that is. Of course it would be no use trying to be too well behaved. The Hub would know from previous experience that Gerry wasn't completely compliant. If his behaviour changed in that way then the Hub would suspect a hidden motive. But, for all the brilliance and intelligence of the Hub, it still couldn't read people's minds…

Gerry decided to investigate the doors again. While he was in the kitchen door F silently closed. The zoo was now officially closed for the night. All visitors were politely asked to leave. Not that there had been any. When he re-entered the main living room he noticed the folding doors were shut again. He shook the handle just to check if they were locked. Not that there was much point. He couldn't get anywhere anyway. Then he checked the bedroom doors and the bathroom. All were unlocked. Finally, with trepidation, he tried the main door, the one that opened into the corridor. To his surprise it was unlocked.

He calmly walked the length of the corridor, and along to his office. That too was open. He checked his desk – nothing seemed out of place. He put on his Holoviewer – the three dimensional vision enhancer and interface. It had been disabled, or at least it was disconnected from the system. He found his tablet on the desk. It too had been disabled. There was an Infopanel on the wall in the kitchen. Normally one could access the full range of online information and services through that. It, too, appeared to be off-line.

As it was practically unheard of for the information systems to go wrong, he doubted that it was a glitch. Clearly whatever role he had been 'chosen' for wasn't going to be very interesting. Moreover, since he had found the door to his office still unlocked, he had begun to hope that he would at least be able to do some private research and writing; but with no connected interfaces he wasn't going to be able to do anything.

Gerry showed very little sign of the irritation he was beginning to feel. He began to hunt around for anything else that might be useful. He looked in drawers and cupboards. Nothing. Then he remembered that he had some paper and a pencil in a box of curios in his old apartment. If the removers had done their job correctly, the box would be in a similar spot in his new apartment.

He ran back down the corridor and into his bedroom. The box was in the right place, on top of a wardrobe. Feverishly now, he found a chair to stand on and lifted down the box. Sure enough, there it was, a twenty five page lined note pad and a propelling pencil.

He remembered the sense of anxiety he had felt as a child, when he couldn't find his box of toys. He had been six and his mother had cleared the lounge ready for a visitor. Gerry had not been informed – or at least, he hadn't been paying attention when she mentioned it. Consequently he assumed that the absence of his box was permanent. Of all his treasured possessions, paper and pencils ranked highly. He hadn't used such outdated technology for more than twenty years. He wasn't even sure if he could remember how to write, but that was unimportant. The great thing was the tools were still there. For several moments he just held them. His pulse began to slow, his breathing eased. The panic dissipated.

The next thing was to make sure that he could hide them somewhere where the cleaner operatives wouldn't find them. One of the Prime Directives related to the sanctity of human privacy. Consequently there would be no surveillance cameras in his bedroom or bathroom. Anywhere else there might be. And cleaner bots, as they were affectionately known, sometimes tidied things away. If they didn't recognise an object they were liable to put them in the trash. Gerry sat down on the end of his bed and started to make a list.

Chapter 14

Carl finally spoke.

"OK I'll be perfectly honest with you. What we are considering is whether there should be a change in one or more of the Prime Directives."

This announcement was met with silence. So far the Prime Directives had always been sacrosanct. There had been a few modifications in the early days but since then none had been changed.

"We're not sure if it would be possible – not in practice."

"Why?" asked Ed.

"Well, we can re-write them alright, but over the years they have become embedded in artificial intelligence networks all across the world. We can't predict exactly what the result would be of changing them in the root repository."

"Do you mean they won't be copied properly?" Max felt a question was needed, so he asked one.

"Not exactly. If we change a directive in the root, and it propagates across the several billion devices that are connected to the Hub, some of them might interpret the new information as an attempt to hack the system. They might consider the sender hub to be alien and cut off the connection."

"Surely there must be a process for this – sending out warning messages, providing an authentication protocol, that sort of thing?"

The French PM was revealing more technological knowledge than anyone had ever accused him of having before…

"Well, that would make sense – *if*, and only if, changes to the PDs were anticipated. But they never were. So there's no protocol."

"That's the first problem." Carl summarised. He gave a little grin as a form of reassurance. It didn't seem to impress anyone else any more than it did himself.

"Oh God! – what's next?"

"Well Ed, the next problem is much more complex. The way that the 563 Prime Directives…"

"How many?!"

Ed had never heard how many there were before, or at least he had never paid attention. Probably neither Jacques nor Max had either, but they weren't so used to displaying their ignorance as Eddie was… and they sure weren't about to start now.

"563. Anyway, the way that the Hub adapts its neural networks to accommodate them and real world data is broadly unknown. If one of the PD's changes, its impact on billions of unknown contexts would be completely unpredictable."

"OK – so why raise this subject at all?"

Eddie was used to getting quickly to the chase and, so far as he could see, there wasn't one to get to.

"Well" Carl was using measured tones again; "we think that as things stand we are headed for a disaster which currently the Hub cannot avert."

Carl paused in case anyone wanted to say something. There was stunned silence.

"OK, it's like this. One Prime Directive assures the sanctity of valid human life, number 1."

"Valid? What the heck does that mean?"

"You're valid if you've not been deactivated."

"So, *deacts* don't count?" Ed was seeking clarification.

"Yes, that's right." Carl sounded cautious. "But is also applies to people without a PIDAC."

"What do we care about that?"

"Well Ed, that accounts for about six billion human beings – the whole population of the East. Now they haven't exactly been ignored by the Hub so far. That's because there is another directive which protects resources that are essential to valid humans' lives and, since we get a significant proportion of our resources from the East, that gives them some form of secondary protection."

"So they're OK then."

Clearly Eddie didn't really care whether they were OK or not but he was at least sensitive to the concerns of others in the room.

"For the time being. But if the Hub perceives them as being a threat – which it would do if things turn critical – then all bets are off."

There was a long pause while the group tried to assimilate this new information. None of them had really given the subject any real thought before. Why would they? Everything had worked ok so far and the Prime Directives were just accepted. No one had ever really questioned them or their validity.

"So this brings us back to model 5 in our feasibility models. You remember that model 5 was the last ditch model. What you won't know is the detail. Models 1 to 4 all involved some form of alteration of our interaction with the East. Trade agreements, health service provision, food supplies, sharing of technical know-how. Models 1 to 3 are cooperative. '*Do it our way, you can see it makes sense.*' Model 4 is coercive – there are threats of military action if East nations don't comply."

"OK, so what about number five?" Ed was still keen to get to the point.

But no one in the room was ready for the answer Carl was about to give to that question.

Chapter 15

Avril was enjoying her new apartment. She had bought some flowers and arranged them in the hallway. She had checked her food preferences and viewed all the new stock in the fridge and food cupboard. She had updated her calendar so that the cleaner-bot would only work when she was out of the apartment.

Various memorabilia had been arranged around the place, to remind her of happy holidays and family events. And she had had time to put in a video call to her mother living in Alexandria – yet another brief monologue which Avril had to curtail rather brusquely. She sat down with a glass of Chardonnay and concluded that she was going to be very happy here.

Somewhere, thousands of miles away, a bunch of electrons were arranging themselves in a certain way that when applied to the chips they were entering, caused an alert to be raised by the Hub. Such complex and indecipherable events happened all around the globe all the time. But this one set of events was particularly important – to Avril. But she would know nothing about it until the next morning. That night she slept well. Her dreams were light and, on waking reflection, amusing. She had her usual breakfast and set off for work at the usual time.

The car took a slightly different route. That was not unusual – it had access to all the traffic information for the whole state, and would quickly calculate and recalculate the optimal route. She entered the building and was cleared through the ID check. On her virtual desk there was the normal number of new files to process. By about 11 am she had got halfway through the pile, which brought her to another status demotion order. The court had granted the order at 1am local time. She had been peacefully sleeping at that point.

Idly, Avril leafed through the documentation. Something caught her attention. The subject of the order was a human – a valid human. Female. 32 yrs of age – the same as Avril. Apparently it was being demoted because it had shown evidence of an unusual and rare gene sequence. This made it of more interest to the Hub as a research sample than in its day job.

This much Avril could deduce from the documents. She paid no attention to the technical reference to the gene sequence. She noticed only that it referred to a "(OR) superfamily" and mentioned "Hyperosmia", which was not a word she knew. This sequence had been discovered, by the Hub, to be associated with two intriguing features. One was the apparent increased resistance to damage by radiation. The other was a highly enhanced sense of smell.

Chapter 16

The first thing Gerry wrote, in a rather shaky childish hand, was the date. He stared at his writing for a moment. His hand-writing always had been spidery, but it seemed strange looking at it again now that he was so much older. It was like looking in the mirror and seeing an image from the past. Without access to the system he couldn't know what the date was. There were no clocks or watches in his world...

He only had 50 sides to write on, so he was going to have to be frugal. This was clearly not the time for rambling reflections on the meaning of life, nor for starting that novel that he was sure he could write if he put his mind to it! No, he was going to need to gather facts, information that could help him understand what was happening, and even help him escape. Although for all his life so far, every door, every vehicle, every transaction had been controlled by the Hub, he had never felt imprisoned. In reality of course he had been. But now he felt it.

He had already deduced that he was not chosen for his intelligence, and probably not for his academic record. Although that had been outstanding, the fact that his access to the system had been cut off made it pretty clear that his future was not going to be an intellectual one. He listed the facts of the past two days as accurately as he could recall them. Some events he could recall to the minute. Others were more vague.

'*no idea why I have been chosen...*' he scribbled.

He tried to recall his doctoral thesis and master's thesis, to see if there might be anything in them that might have caught the Hub's attention. But it couldn't be that, otherwise his network privileges wouldn't have been curtailed. He tried to recall his behaviour over the past few months, in case he had behaved anti-socially. But he knew it couldn't be that, because he would have been warned or even received a trial.

There was no point in accused persons being brought to a trial in person. The Hub would already have had more than enough evidence. And observational data about the accused would have been amassed from every conceivable source, to create a profile of the person. From that it would be a statistical almost certainty that the person was either guilty or innocent of the alleged offence. So why waste time, and money, with an actual trial? However, for the record, documents had to be assembled, admitted, checked and then archived – in case there was an appeal. So if he had not been served with notice of a trial result, he couldn't have been accused of an offence – and therefore there was no opportunity for an appeal. So why was he here – as an exhibit?

For a moment he half wondered if he were the victim of a practical joke. Such things had happened before – not to him, but to people he knew. Generally they were people connected with security or personnel screening – where their mates might have opportunity to raise a temporary 'concern'. Such things could be erased locally and there would be no harm done. But Gerry didn't know anyone with that kind of privilege. So perhaps it was malicious! But again he racked his brain for a likely candidate and drew another blank.

Then he started to analyse his situation. Two days ago he had been a research scientist in biology. Highly paid and highly respected. He had fifteen or more projects on the go and was expected to be producing useful results by the end of the month. His supervisor had been entirely happy with his work and had been talking about Gerry's potential career path.

Gerry was happy at the Smithsonian. He liked Washington; it always seemed to him to be a clean city, well planned. He enjoyed the symbolism of the buildings. His uncle was buried in the Arlington cemetery, with full military honours. It felt like home to him. So he wasn't that keen on a career move that might take him thousands of miles away. Maybe he had let his reluctance show? But surely incarceration was a bit of a harsh punishment for that! No, whichever way his mind turned, it just could not come up with an explanation. The last fact on his list so far was '*now in an enclosure. I seem to have become an exhibit!*' There was an attempt at humour in the remark, but Gerry didn't feel it.

Chapter 17

Carl leaned back on the desk behind him, indicating the seriousness of what he was about to say. He hesitated for a moment and drew a large breath, biting the corner of his lower lip.

"Model 5 is final. It proposes the complete elimination of the Eastern countries' populations."

There was another lengthy pause. Eyes moved from one person to another, seeking some indication of the owners' emotion.

"So, Carl, let me see if I have understood this."

 Max finally broke the ice.

"You and your team have come up with 5 models, four of which have been trialed to some extent, but none of those four shows any sign of being successful. The fifth is clearly completely unacceptable and probably impractical any way."

"So far you've got it, yes."

"But these are your models – not the Hub's?"

"Correct."

"So if we don't like them we just remove them."

"Certainly – we can't tell the Hub what to do in any case. They were just models – hypothetical."

"So I don't see the problem."

"Ah, well, there is a problem. The thing is, when I say that we came up with the models, that doesn't fully describe the situation. We didn't exactly write them out of thin air. We set down the broad picture, the situation as we saw it. Then we got the Hub to run the numbers and suggest various scenarios. As you might expect it came up with several thousand. So by introducing some extra constraints we managed to get the result list down to five – the ones you now know about."

"Sorry, I still don't see the problem."

Carl's slightly lengthy intake of breath belied his disarming smile. He was becoming impatient.

"The problem is this. We used the Hub to run a what-if analysis. It told us what it would do. So what we have now is not just a set of potential models. It's also a set of predictions of what the Hub would do if those starting conditions were to appear in reality. And we believe they are about to appear very soon."

"Oh my God! And there's no way you can just tell the Hub not to execute model five?"

"No."

"So what the hell can we do? – there must be something, goddammit!"

Eddie had entered the discussion with his usual can-do attitude.

"We think we might be able to alter one of the PDs."

"Which is where we started…"

Max was reminding people of what they already knew. Eddie's eyes rolled heavenward. Jacques was beginning to sweat profusely. Carl and Max exchanged a secretive glance. Max knew more than he was letting on but he and Carl needed to have the other two on board – Jacques because he was chair of the group and Ed because of his family's widespread influence all over the Western world. Jacques was first to break the silence.

"Which PD? And how do you propose altering it? - given what you said earlier about the unpredictability of such an exercise."

Carl took the baton again. His right hand was scratching his balding pate, as if to indicate the extreme complexity of the detail that lay behind the layman's description he was conjuring up.

"Well we propose doing the same kind of exercise that we did before. Ask the Hub to come up with predictions based on the changes we might make to the PDs."

"Well let's get on with it then!"

Eddie was getting more impatient by the minute.

"We would, were it not for the fact that there is no protocol for mapping changes to the PDs. In other words we can't be sure that all the Hubs would see this as hypothetical. The risk is that one or more might see this as a real attempt to change a PD and start a defensive chain reaction."

Eddie hit his forehead with his hand. From the volume of the smack it was pretty clear that it must have hurt. He didn't flinch. Carl certainly had his attention.

Chapter 18

Avril was still in work mode, processing the court's judgement. The similarities between the operative being considered and herself had interested her, but not fully made their mark. But her next action was going to bring her face to face with the awful truth. She had now to enter the operative's ID. It wasn't a tiresome action – you just pressed some empty space in front of your head, where the three dimensional image of the document was being presented by Holoview. But it did force her to look at the ID. Twenty four numbers and letters was an awful lot to remember. Few people knew their own ID off by heart. Avril certainly didn't, but she did recognise part of it. Three characters randomly matched her aunt's name, 'liz'. They stood out like a Christmas tree.

At first, Avril still only thought of it as a chance coincidence. So, out of interest more than concern, she got her ID card out of her bag. With PIDACs you didn't need an old fashioned card. But it was sometimes useful to actually have the number in front of you. She rotated the card round to the right position. She chuckled at the ancient photo of herself, taken ten years before. Then she looked at the numbers. It was a perfect match.

"Oh my God! Oh God – I'm being asked to sign my own warrant!"

She shouted. She could shout as loudly as she liked. No one was going to hear, since she was alone in her office, and all the offices were sound-proofed. In a state of panic, she rapidly did the required checks – not so as to finish the task quickly, but in order to find some error in the case. She went over the documents a second time. Then she sat down at her desk and broke down. She was still slumped over her desk, sobbing, when the cleaner-bot came in to do its rounds.

The Hub had learned about distress and knew that it was best to give someone in this condition a wide birth. It didn't want to be attacked! She was still slumped over her desk when the bot left, having tentatively picked up the sodden tissues from the floor. The Hub had already noted Avril's distress and had analysed her work-load for the day, and had come to the rather obvious conclusion that her work had upset her. As she seemed to be severely distressed, the Hub ordered a medic to her office. An hour later she was in a hospital bed under the blissful influence of a sedative. Meanwhile her task remained undone.

The workload monitor had noted that this particular document had stayed in Avril's office for an unreasonably long time, so the case was automatically assigned to someone else. That someone else was working in an office 13,000 miles away. She had no knowledge of Avril or her situation. So there was no reason to hesitate in giving the order the all clear. Avril had gone to sleep in a hospital. She would wake in a zoo.

Chapter 19

"So, what the hell are you going to do?"

Eddie slammed his fist on the table. He was not used to situations that encouraged indecision. Normally he would be presented with an executive summary by his secretary. A couple of people might discuss technical details, which he was not expected to understand. Then they would look to him to ratify their decision and that would be it.

Eddie prided himself on never taking more than thirty seconds to make an important decision. He reckoned he got it right more than half the time. That's all it needed. Speed was essential because, if you'd made the wrong decision, the quicker you got on with it the quicker you'd get to your next right decision. And the more right decisions you make, the more money you make. But this farce had already taken up two hours of his precious time.

Carl drew on his increasingly white beard. He walked behind his chair and placed his hands on its back so as to lean forward.

"What we are proposing is a rather subtle change to one PD. Currently there is a PD which states that the survival of samples of a species that contains rare genetic material is secondary to the survival of valid humans, but more important than any other PDs. That ensures that we don't lose ancient or valuable DNA. Our zoos keep samples with these DNA strains alive while we do further research and start the cloning process. When we have a number of viable embryos or seeds or whatever, they are frozen. At that point the original sample is no longer such a high priority."

"Can't see how that's gonna help much!"

"Well Eddy", Carl was trying not to be patronising but was clearly losing the battle with himself – "the Hub knows that there are six billion non-valid humans along with countless billions of other uncharted organisms out there in the East. But it discounts them because it doesn't know anything about them. What we propose doing is to make the Hub default to assuming that humans it doesn't know about may contain such rare genes unless it knows otherwise. That will prevent it from being able to action model five – hopefully."

"Lovely word, hopefully!" Jacques was pretending to savour it. Max assumed that this was how the French did sarcasm. If one looked carefully one would see the slightest hint of a smile on Max's face.

"And if your hopes are unrealised?"

"Then we don't know what will happen."

"So it's Russian roulette!"

"Pretty much."

"Oh great!"

Chapter 20

The thing that really frustrated Gerry was being cut off from the system. Normally he'd be able to access the world's databanks and get his DNA analysed. From that he would probably have been able to discover why exactly he had had the dubious honour of being 'chosen'. It would have taken no longer than half an hour. As it was he had absolutely no chance of ever discovering the reason. His only chance would be if he, at some time in his research, had happened to read the relevant material, and also had seen, and memorised, the relevant part of his own genome.

The twenty three chromosomes in his own genetic makeup ran to three billion base pairs. For him to draw the right conclusion was like finding a needle in a haystack, but a haystack with more bits of hay than all the stars in the known universe.

Gerry mused on the prospect of rehearsing all this factual irrelevance over and over again for the rest of his captive life – however long that might be. With a reflective sniff he dismissed the thought. He had excellent thought control so he wouldn't be wasting time and energy on imponderables. Of course he was completely unaware that at this very moment, four of the most powerful men on the planet were considering tinkering with the very foundations of Gerry's world in a way that might have profound effects on his life.

Their tinkering would also have potentially enormous effects on Avril's life, not to mention on those of the eight billion other people on the planet.

Avril awoke unaware of all that. She hadn't even heard of the Zurich group. Very few people had. And those that did know anything about it were almost all wrong. The Zurich group had a powerful PR department sending out very effective mis-information. What she was aware of though, was that she was not at home. Slowly her memory of the previous day – if it indeed had been the previous day – came back to her. She had found out her fate. She had collapsed. She vaguely remembered the para-med bot lifting her gently and putting her into an ambulance. After that it was all a blur.

She looked around, to try to identify the paraphernalia of a hospital. But there was none. In some ways the place looked familiar. Wasn't that her favourite flower vase on the side? Did she not recognise the novel on the coffee table? But she knew that she wasn't in her apartment. The colours were wrong. But especially the smell was wrong. She resolved to ask the next nurse or staff member she saw just what was going on and immediately set to planning her questions.

There was a symmetry between Avril and Gerry. They were both now imprisoned in a zoo because of a rare genetic variation. She had seen the documentation for both of them. No doubt the gene reference had been in front of her. No doubt the technical description of the suspected phenomenological impact of their uniqueness had been in plain sight too. But it all meant nothing to her.

Gerry knew none of this, and it would have meant everything to him!

Chapter 21

"I'm not happy with this."

The French PM was smoothing the back of his head, revealing his tension.

"You're proposing a fundamental change, which has never been done before, without a formal protocol, AND you don't know if it will work. And by whose authority?"

Max fielded the legal questions.

"The thing is, as you all know, there is no authority for what we do." Occasionally his eyebrows would twitch involuntarily giving the impression of being mildly surprised by his own statement.

"Formally we don't do anything – just talk. No records are kept. No one audits us. We just make sure that things get done properly. And you have to admit it's a system that's worked pretty well for a hundred years or so!"

"I can't argue with that."

"I sense a 'but' Jacques?"

"Yes – it's worked alright for us, in the West. But I doubt if those in the East would agree so easily."

"They always have the chance to come on board!"

It seemed that Jacques was beginning to get a conscience about the state of the vast majority of earth's human population, a majority that he and the other members of the group had been entirely happy to ignore before. Eddie was not so troubled.

"I think we're wasting time here. The East depends on us protecting the planet for them just as much as for our world. They wouldn't know where to start. We need to get on with it."

Carl entered the conversation again.

"I know we're not in a perfect situation for making a decision but what I've told you is the best we've got. We've all got where we are by being able to make tough decisions, take risks, shoulder responsibility."

Ed was nodding in agreement.

"So, what we're asking for is your agreement, in principle, to this approach. There is a lot of detail to sort out and, of course, formally it's an IDIC action."

"Can we consult the other members of the group?" Jacques was being the voice of reason.

"No" Max replied, "this group has always proceeded on the understanding that it's the members who turn up who – what shall I say – conclude a discussion."

He nearly said 'make the decision' but of course formally the group never made any decisions. For a while no one spoke.

Max broke the silence;

"Well I think this conversation is concluded." His hand was already fetching his sunglasses. Ed helped himself to another sugary cake and they all departed without another word.

Chapter 22

Gerry's list wasn't progressing as quickly as he had hoped. So far he had barely covered one page. His attention wandered following his gaze around the room. The paintwork was perfect. You'd have to examine the cutting in with a magnifier to detect any imperfections. The colours were evenly applied. The carpet was new and clean, a neutral flecked grey. For a moment he started drawing the room. He stopped himself and recovered his thoughts. He emptied the pencil leads from the bright red body onto his desk and counted them. There were six.

As he recalled, it wasn't the writing that did the most damage to the leads. It was the way they would break off when you weren't concentrating – press a little too hard and the end would fly off at some speed. That would be a millimetre gone.

In the day when people used pencils it was hardly a problem – just a minor irritation. You could always buy more, for just a few pence. Now of course it was a major problem. So far as he could remember, there were no spares to be found anywhere in his box of nostalgia. He was determined to write very carefully!

He looked around the room. So far he had found plenty of good food to eat and even some reasonable wine. The welcome bottle had been finished the first night, but there were always two bottles of red in the store, and a couple of white in the fridge. He wondered whether there were any rules about his provisions – were they rewards for some kind of behaviour? Was he in an experiment? Or was he just being preserved as a gene pool, like many of the other exhibits.

His mind went back to a childhood memory of a zoo, when conditions were less humane. One animal, a polar bear, was kept in a space that was far too small for it and without any kind of stimulation. The bear used to pace, vigorously, up and down, day after day. It was a decade before Gerry learnt the psychology that allowed him to interpret the bear's behaviour as insanity. He wondered how long he would last before going similarly mad. He wondered if that was the experiment. Perhaps that thought could drive him to resist its onset. Or perhaps just that thought, or one of an unknown number of similar ones, would actually drive him insane. That was why he needed to make the list, he told himself. But still nothing came into his head.

By way of a change, he glanced across the walkway to the chimp opposite. It was enjoying a banana. Its eyes would look up and across at Gerry for a moment, then back down at the fruit. It would scratch an itch, without apparently being concerned about its cause. Suddenly it was off, careering around the enclosure with speed and ease.

Gerry wondered if it knew any form of sign language. Some of the specimens in the zoo had been in language experiments, he knew that. He knew the major signs of one of the languages that had been used. He thought perhaps he might engage this chimp in a conversation; but so far he had been completely unable to attract the animal's attention. It seemed to look right through Gerry.

Gerry reflected on the fragility of communication. Then, quite unexpectedly, he felt a sense of rage welling up inside him. The coffee mug was in his hand and, without thinking, he threw it against the glass wall of his prison. It shattered into fragments. Dribbles of coffee ran slowly down the glass, eventually forming a brown pool on the new carpet. He had expected the chimp to be startled by the noise. In Gerry's enclosure it was quite deafening. The chimp clearly didn't notice a thing.

Chapter 23

Max drove himself back to the airport and handed the car back to the mysterious security guard who, like a dozen others, were sworn to secrecy about their job.

"Merci monsieur." The words were brief and accompanied by a kind but small smile.

They were all recruited from the Swiss Guard. Suitable candidates would have served at the Vatican for at least five years and would therefore be extremely experienced in dealing with highly confidential and secret matters. They were the epitome of discretion.

It would be another ex-Swiss Guard who would meet him at his next destination. In this case the recruitment process was highly informal. No one in the Zurich group, apart from Carl, knew anything about the operation. Max was walking an extremely thin and dangerous tight-rope.

His private jet landed at the Indira Gandhi International Airport in New Delhi just eight hours later. An indistinct black saloon car drove out onto the tarmac to meet him. The ex-Swiss Guard wore black trousers, a black polo neck and a Chinese collar jacket. The combination was very fashionable that year. Nobody would give Gabriel a second look. Max had chosen Gabriel partly because his obviously Italian name wasn't as obvious as some others.

"Ciao..." the two men embraced briefly. Max was used to trusting Gabriel with his life. Such trust created a strong bond. Max's mission in Delhi was infinitely more secret than his previous one in Zurich. He was going to the East. And a lot depended on it. The future of the East's six billion people was in his hands, it seemed. He wondered how it had happened.

He had been born in London, educated in England and entered the Civil Service immediately after graduation. In a way the job had found him. He had been walking the streets of Oxford, supposedly revising for his finals, when he felt a hand on his shoulder. Its owner was a well-dressed man in his forties. He was carrying a leather briefcase.

"Max, you don't know me but I wonder if you could spare me a minute."

"What? – who? – what's going on?"

Max was young enough to be utterly phased by the experience of being recognised and named by a complete stranger. Something in the back of his mind was trying to warn him. *You don't know this person. He could be dangerous. It might be a con.*

But on the other hand, the man looked very respectable, and was well spoken. Another part of Max's mind was experiencing flattery – and liked it. They walked to the park just around the corner and sat on the bench. The man was careful checking out the park. The bench was a long way from any bushes, isolated in the middle of the lawn, so there was little chance of an eavesdropper being within earshot.

"Max, we've been aware of you for a while now. My colleagues and I have noticed your contributions to your college debating society, we've seen your contributions to the political journals, and we've checked out your background. All that we have seen so far makes us think that you might do well to work with us."

"Um – that's very nice, but who are you exactly?"

Max was feeling more uncomfortable by the minute. He half expected to be bundled into the boot of a car, or walked away with a gun in his back. He had seen all this stuff in the movies…

"Oh, I'm sorry; I should have introduced myself. I'm Charles."

They shook hands. Max was none the wiser.

"I'd like you to meet some of my people. See if you can get to the Carlton in London on Saturday, will you. 4pm – in time for tea. Show this card at the door and you'll be let in."

With that the man was gone. It clearly wasn't an invitation. It was an order. Whether Max went or not merely depended on whether he would choose to accept the authority that lay behind the order.

He arrived at the Carlton early so he took a turn around the block a few times to fill the time. He didn't want to appear too keen. In his hand was the card that the mysterious man had given him. It bore a logo of some sort. Max had never seen anything quite like it before. It pictured an eagle standing on a pyramid. Max assumed that the pyramid was connected with free-masonry but he didn't know how the eagle fitted into the picture. The peculiar thing was that there were no words, no telephone number, no email address, none of the things you might expect on a business card of the time.

At the club he presented it to the stone faced concierge. The man stiffened slightly as if he suddenly realised that rather more respect was due to the young man than he had at first expected.

"This way please sir."

He was led to a low lit minor meeting room, sumptuously decorated, and shown to a leather arm chair. A waiter, unbidden, appeared with a range of single malt whiskeys. Max chose one at random, having no knowledge of the mystical art. Then he was left alone, for a long five minutes. Finally one of the doors into the lounge opened quietly and in walked the stranger whom he had met in Oxford.

"Ah Max!" he said in a clipped upper class accent.

Max's own accent certainly wasn't vulgar, but it was a long way from this rarefied tone.

78

"Good of you to come. There's a couple of chaps here I'd like you to meet."

Max found the chumminess of it all quite endearing. He didn't know what he was getting himself into but he rather thought he was going to like it.

"How has your last term been? I know that you're expected to get a first and that some people hope that you will do a doctorate." That was news to Max.

"We think that you might be well advised to forego all that time wandering around the dusty corridors of academia - and get straight into the workplace."

Max didn't know what to say. Charles, meanwhile, was looking at the door, clearly waiting for someone.

Chapter 24

Avril waited and waited for a nurse but none came. Gradually she began to feel brave enough to explore. Avril was not the kind of person to take unilateral action. She was comforted by the security of following rules or instructions. But right now she didn't know any relevant rules and there didn't seem to be any instructions. Slowly she pulled back the sheet and dropped her long legs neatly to the floor. As she gradually oriented herself in her second new home in as many days, she noticed some strange smells.

She had always had an extraordinary sense of smell. As a child she was forever asking her mother what this or that flower was and how beautiful it smelt."

"Don't be silly dear; they don't smell!"

Eventually she stopped remarking on the smells. No one else seemed to notice most of the ones that she noticed, and she began to wonder if she were imagining things. However, when she started studying biochemistry her rather special talent brought a certain amount of fame. She could detect the presence of chemicals in the lab at a distance of five or ten metres. She quickly became a lab assistant, which earned her some precious extra pocket money and various privileges. She also had the advantage that she could tell if people had left the tops off flasks or bottles just by inhaling. She became a bit of a legend - and the butt of many affectionate jokes.

She quickly found her way to L&S Berkeley where she excelled. Although she was fairly attractive, she fought off admirers with an element of disdain. 'Men you can find anywhere; education like this you can't.' However, in her final year she finally succumbed to a post-grad from Boalt, the law school. And although she never fell in love with him, she fell head over heels with his subject, and exchanged a dazzling career in science for a mediocre one in law. She was recalling her unpredictable career path as she explored her new home.

She was still in shock and not really grasping her new situation. In this dazed state was able to think more reflectively than normal. She explored the kitchen and made herself a hot chocolate. She sat down, and waited. *Surely someone will come and tell me what's going on?* Part of her was still acting the part of a hospital patient and she assumed that there would be readings to be taken. But no one came. She tried to put in a call to her mother but the comms were down.

Gradually the reality dawned on her. Her spirits sank and she started gently sobbing. She was on her own and she wanted her mummy.

Chapter 25

After a while Gerry calmed down. He picked up the pieces of broken mug and put them in the trash. He looked through the glass wall and, ignoring the chimp, looked further down the corridor at the cells either side of the chimp. 'Cells' – that was the word. 'Enclosure' might be technically the right term to use in a zoo – but that would be a normal zoo. Zoos that kept free humans against their well – they were prisons. He was in a cell. So ran his train of thoughts.

Of course he didn't realise that his status had been demoted to 'retained'. He merely thought of himself as being chosen. He believed he still had all the rights and privileges of a valid operative. Only, that he had been incarcerated for a reason that was, as yet, unknown to him. As a free man he felt imprisoned.

To the right of the chimp's enclosure was a similar one, though he had not yet seen an occupant. From what he remembered, from when he was free to walk on the other side of the glass, all the animals in this area were chimps or apes. Though, now he thought of it, he did recall a couple of them being unoccupied. The glass observation window of several of them had revealed nothing because behind them there had been full height and width metal doors.

Of course! – his cell was one of them. There was another, he recalled, the other side! He turned his gaze to the left of the chimp's. Yes, that too had a closed metal door behind it. Maybe there was a new occupant in that one too. Gerry hoped that whatever it was, it would know some sign language.

Chapter 26

Charles introduced the other three men who had just entered the room. They were all confident, impeccably dressed and very well spoken. Max doubted if he would remember their names for more than a minute or two. He wasn't interested in names. He wanted to know what this was all about!

"Mr Brunner…"

A tall, rather weedy man was speaking. His mouth carried an equally weedy-looking moustache. From its discolouration Max presumed he was a smoker.

" .. you are probably a bit mystified by all this. Let me put you in the picture." He looked around the gathering; "Shall I be mother?"

He picked up the whiskey decanter and offered it round. Charles allowed him to fill his glass to the brim.

"We represent an organisation which has global interests. That organisation needs from time to time to acquire new, ah, fresh blood, shall we say – to keep us up to date with developments. We think you might make a good candidate."

The weedy man stopped, looking as though he was satisfied that he had answered all of Max's questions. Max began to realise that he was not powerless in this situation.

"What organisation?"

"Ah, well, we really can't go into that kind of detail here. What we need to know is whether you might consider going to the next stage."

"Which is?"

"We'd like you to spend a weekend with us – so we can get to know each other a bit better; so we can find out a bit more about your interests and ambitions – see if they match up, you know the sort of thing."

Max certainly didn't know – though he thought he could imagine.

"But, tell us first, what are your views on world population?"

Suddenly the drinks party had changed into a kind of interview. Max tried to remind himself that he didn't have to be here, didn't have to answer any questions. It was up to *them* to say who they were and what they wanted.

"Tell me – are you members of the conservative party?"

It seemed a natural question, given the location and the whole tone of the meeting.

"Oh, goodness no! This is just a convenient meeting place. I mean, we might individually be members – have to be, I suppose, to get in here!"

The others all laughed. It seemed like an in-joke.

"But we're not here representing the conservative party, if that's what you mean. We don't represent any political party. Our organisation is strictly non-political."

"So, are you MI5, MI6, GCHQ?..."

"No, no..." he laughed thinly "nothing like that. We're not recruiting spies!"

Max thought that although this was probably not a lie, it was certainly less than the truth.

"The thing is, our organisation is a sort of international charity, looking out for the good of humanity, that sort of thing."

The man's attempt to be 'old boy' was hardly convincing. The others were staring at Max with intense concentration. All of them had their finger-tips joined. All had eyebrows raised, as if anticipating something.

"So, what do you want with me?"

The man coughed. "We are particularly interested in your career."

Max was surprised. He himself wasn't particularly interested in his career at all and, so far as he was aware, had never given any indication of a leaning to one profession or another. He just assumed that he would find a career that would enable him to become a politician.

"I'm not sure that I know what career to choose."

"That's what makes you interesting. We think we might be able to give you a little direction, a little help. In return for which you might give us a little help."

Some more whiskey was drunk. There was a little general conversation about current political issues. Then the weedy man stood up and shook Max firmly by the hand.

"Goodbye Mr Brunner. It was a pleasure. Thank you for dropping by. We hope we will meet again."

Max correctly took this as a cue to leave. As he left the room, the weedy man extended his hand.

"Your card, if you please?"

Max handed back the mysterious card and walked out of the Carlton for the first and last time. He thought that if that had been an interview he had certainly failed. And he felt no desire to work for whatever shadowy organisation he had just had a glancing contact with. He was certain he would never meet any of them again!

Chapter 27

Avril awoke from a short sleep and found herself curled up in the corner of the room. She was staring at the multi-panelled door which ran all the way across her living room. She wondered why she hadn't really noticed it before.

As she got up, with some unsteadiness, she knocked over the mug of now cold chocolate drink. She cursed. Taking the round handle in her right hand she tried to open the door but it was clearly locked. She explored the other rooms – a kitchen, she'd been in there before; the bathroom, the bedroom. There was a low bedside light and on the bedside table a couple of her favourite books. Exactly where they had been in her previous apartment.

So much was familiar; but so much was very alien. She tried the remaining door, which she assumed must lead into a corridor. It was locked. She looked carefully around the handle to see if there was a catch or lock of some kind. Nothing. Usually doors unlocked themselves automatically as you got near them, if you had clearance to go through.

Had this been her real home, this would have been the main entrance and it would have unlocked itself with a beep. You still had to turn a handle, because security required that you be able to refuse someone entry if you didn't know them. This door didn't beep and the handle wouldn't turn.

So this was what demotion meant. Although she knew from the documents she had seen, that she was being demoted to 'retained', she hadn't really known what to expect. But what she had expected was that someone would talk to her – give her a briefing, prepare her for her new life. To calm the rising sense of panic she was feeling, she sat on the floor and started practising her yoga exercises. Within minutes her mind was somewhere else, somewhere calm, somewhere safe.

Chapter 28

Max returned to Oxford and soon forgot about his meeting with the strange spooks at the Carlton. He assumed they were spooks, despite their denial. He completed his studies with moderate success – his dissertation had lacked some of the brilliance that had marked his earlier work – but he wasn't particularly worried. His tutors assured him there would be no lack of takers for his talent.

Near the end of the term, corporate employers came to the university to show their wares. Max wouldn't have bothered except that he bumped into a complete stranger that morning. To be precise, she had bumped into him. She was exceedingly pretty, exactly Max's type. Her eyes twinkled as she steered him towards a cup of coffee and before he knew it they were attending the milk round.

There were probably a hundred or more stands, nearly all 'manned' by pretty girls, smiling sweetly and trying to engage the students' interest. Max passed by the banks, the pharmaceuticals, the energy companies, the software giants; he even noticed the security services' stalls, and smiled slightly, recalling that day at the Carlton.

Then he found himself strangely drawn to a stand that had no company name, no self-acclaiming straplines or colourful banners. No pretty girls even. There were simply two impeccably dressed men and a logo. Nothing else. The logo had an irresistible magnetic affect on Max. It was in the form of a pyramid, topped by an eagle. One of the men stretched out his hand to Max.

"Mr Brunner – how good to see you again."

The man handed Max a card. It had a date and a location written on it, and nothing else.

"We do hope you'll come along Max. It will be a very interesting weekend for you. Only," the man hesitated while he ensured that he had Max's full attention "please don't tell anyone about this."

Max took the card and walked on, slightly scared. When he was out of sight the two men rapidly dismantled the stall and took its contents away in a large black carry-all. Max hunted around for the girl who had taken him there but there was no sign of her.

Chapter 29

Gerry realised that had been staring at the cell for ages. It wasn't a decision he'd made, to wait for the doors to open, but that was what he was doing. Over the next six hours or so, he kept finding himself doing it again; a bit like people at the sea-side – staring out into the emptiness of the ocean, apparently waiting for something to happen. Actually he wasn't looking when the door finally did open. He had been in the kitchen, preparing some food for later. Most of the day had gone by and soon his own viewing doors would close. He had given up expecting to see the new exhibit. No doubt it would appear tomorrow.

He poured himself a glass of wine. In many ways this new life of his was a kind of nirvana. Endless supplies of food that he didn't have to earn. A spacious apartment which he didn't have to service or clean. More wine than he could ever finish. No work to do. But on the other hand, there really was nothing to do at all! Except watch that cell opposite.

He returned to his large room. To his surprise the doors that had remained steadfastly shut while he had observed them, had contrarily decided to open when his back was turned. He expected to see another chimp or ape. That was mostly what was kept in this section of the zoo. But as it was he could see nothing.

However, the contents of the cell were altogether different from those of its neighbour. The chimp opposite had fake trees and bushes and some odd shaped objects that people obviously thought chimps would like. This new cell was not like that at all. In fact it was almost exactly the same as his own.

Gerry's heart missed several beats. Another human! Perhaps one that could speak English – not that speaking would help. Maybe someone who could read English – he had paper and pencil, he could write large messages and they could communicate. It would be a bit of a one-sided conversation though, since probably the other person would not have anything to write on.

For a moment he thought about his Holoviewer – perhaps the new 'resident' would have one. They might be disconnected from the Hub but they would usually still communicate with one another directly, as long as there was a clear path for the signal to communicate over. But then he remembered. The glass window behind which he and his new colleague were imprisoned, was coated with a single atom layer of aluminium. It was designed to block radio waves. They had told him about this at his indoctrination when he joined the zoo. Captive animals also had chips and in order to ensure that there was no unexpected behavioural interference caused by them being activated by another exhibit's chip, all cells were electromagnetically isolated from each other. That was what they had said. Gerry was beginning to wonder if he had been given the truth!

Ten minutes later Gerry was still staring at the apparently empty cell when his doors starting closing. As the panels unfolded, cutting off an increasing proportion of his three metre wide window, he edged his way sideways, so as to continue to get a view, hoping to see who or what his new fellow prisoner was. Only at the last minute, when there was about a centimetre gap left, did he see a movement. He caught sight of what looked like a woman. And then the view disappeared.

Chapter 30

Avril's yoga had been very effective. In the past she had been known to enter such a detached state that the phone could ring, or the kettle boil, or even someone enter the room without her noticing. Indeed the intensity of her trance-like state seemed to be proportional to the stress level of the situation she was trying to escape. So this day also. She had probably never been in such a stressful and terrifying situation and yet now she was almost dead to world, which accounted for the fact that when her viewing window finally opened, she was entirely oblivious to it.

It had been open for nearly two hours by the time she came out of her meditation and by then she was so relaxed that she scarcely gave the fact any attention. She walked over to the window and her attention was attracted by a movement on the other side of the walkway. A door was closing in the room opposite. She caught a brief glimpse of a man's shape.

Whereas Gerry had seen the vision of a nearly identical room as holding all sorts of terrors, Avril merely felt comforted. Another room like hers, another person. It was going to be OK, as long as they were allowed to meet and talk.

Her attention then strayed to the cell next door, the one opposite her. That was empty, apart from a tree and some bushes. This seemed strange to her. At first she had assumed that she was seeing into an apartment on the other side of the street. Gradually she began to comprehend that this was not a street and the rooms were not apartments. The 'street' that separated her from the room opposite was only a matter of a few feet wide. She looked up and saw there was a roof over it. It reminded her of some quaint old shopping arcade she had visited once.

But these windows did not reveal shop interiors. One was like hers, a kind of apartment. However, the one opposite and its neighbour too, were empty and looked more like cells at the zoo. She saw her reflection in the window opposite and idly started combing her hair with her fingers. She strained her neck to see more windows, further down the corridor. Without exception they, too, looked just like enclosures at the zoo. 'Oh well,' she thought, 'an office in a zoo isn't so bad.' But then the word 'retained' came back to her. Suppose she weren't working in a zoo now. Suppose she was merely one of the exhibits! She rejected that thought with a chuckle. Impossible. She went to explore the fridge.

Chapter 31

Max arrived at the address he had been given at four p.m., as directed. It was a country hotel, a converted old rectory. As he entered the front door his taxi drove away behind him and a pretty girl in a smart suit welcomed him.

"Please follow me Mr Brunner."

She had an impeccable accent and stylish deportment, suggesting a good finishing school. At the main desk, another member of staff welcomed him and asked him for his watch, phone and wallet.

"You won't be needing them and we like to ensure that you don't get disturbed in any way while you are here. Please enjoy your stay."

"Oh – can I ask, how long will I be staying?"

The two staff members briefly looked at each other, with a slight smile.

"You can stay as long as you like sir. I'll show you to your room."

He followed the male staff member across the hall and up an enormous Queen Anne staircase. Max loved these impressive staircases. His parents' house had one – it was only a manor house, but a very beautiful one. Compared to some of his fellow students' homes, it was miniscule. His best friend, Rick, had grown up on a 2,000 acre estate, in a 15 bedroom house. But Max always felt that as long as there was a decent staircase, you were OK.

His room was entered by double doors, ornately decorated, and was big enough to take four or five double beds. There was, of course, only one. The view from the leaded diamond windows was breath-taking. A fountain played a few hundred yards away. Peacocks could be seen strutting purposefully. There were immaculately trimmed box hedges and some topiary, and a couple of gardeners could be seen fulfilling their subservient vocation. It was an image from another age, one in which Max felt entirely at home.

He had been invited to come down to the lounge whenever he was ready. Curiosity drove him to making that sooner rather than later, but not before he had attended to his hair and his tie. Everything about Max was always perfect. There were sumptuous chairs, large old portraits, Arabian carpets – everything had a stylish air of age about it. A waiter motioned him to take a seat and then brought a large schooner and set it down beside him.

"Sweet or dry sir?"

Sherry was not Max's usual tipple, but there didn't appear to be anything else on offer so he accepted dry. Very quietly a short, bald and rather rotund man entered the room and introduced himself.

"Ah, you must be Max. I'm Simon. Very pleased to meet you – I've heard a lot about you."

Simon beamed, and extended his hand palm upwards in that very relaxed and supremely confident way that very powerful men do.

"How was your trip? Good?"

Clearly a positive reply was expected, so Max gave him one. He thought better of complaining about the late train and the surly taxi driver and, anyway, he had got there on time in the end.

"Good, good." Simon had the air of someone who would patiently play out the scene of social etiquette 'til the cows came home but was really concentrating on the main item on the agenda.

"We'll wait until the others get here before we get going properly but let me ask you this question."

94

Max wasn't quite sure whether this was an interview or merely small talk and, since he didn't know what it was he might be being interviewed for, decided not to worry about it.

"Of course" he said.

"What was the single most important thing you learnt at Oxford, would you say?"

Max had been studying PPE, with a view to entering politics as his father had done. But also like his father, he intended to have a career first. He couldn't abide these career politicians – they knew nothing of the real world.

"I suppose the most valuable thing would be that people often don't say what they mean – and vice versa."

"Ah – a sceptic!"

"Or a cynic?"

A new voice had entered the room. It was owned by a willowy man with rather overlarge, black-rimmed glasses, now entirely out of fashion. From his bearing Max deduced there might be some military background.

"Max – this is Sir David."

Another confident hand was extended to Max.

"Ah, Max, welcome. Please, call me David."

"So, Max, are you a cynic or a sceptic?"

"I would prefer to be thought sceptical. That implies reasoned argument and research going before judgement. Whereas a cynic comes to the issue with a prejudiced mind."

"Stay around here too long and you'll become a cynic! What!"

Simon laughed loudly at his own joke and clapped Max on the back.

"But what about your views of international politics? Are we making progress or going backwards?"

"I'm not sure that we're doing either, taking the long term view. Political fashions come and go and people who've been around a bit say they've seen it all before."

"They're the cynics! – see, told you so!"

Simon introduced another piece of self-congratulatory humour. Max decided to try to ground the conversation.

"The thing is that people seem doomed to keep making the same mistakes their forebears made. All that changes is the technology."

"Yes, but the technology changes everything, don't you think?"

David was back in the discussion.

"I mean, with modern warfare far fewer people have to be on the ground."

"Yes I agree – in fact we had a demo at college last year…"

He was interrupted swiftly by Simon.

"A demonstration?! – at Oxford?"

"Oh, no, sorry – not a political demonstration. A technical demo, from a team in the CGI department."

"CGI?"

"Computer graphics. They showed us how they could create a five minute news report from a battle zone just using software. No real pictures. No real soldiers."

"I say! – no injuries!"

David was feigning surprise. In reality, he knew all about this stuff. A gong announced that dinner was served. David's eye followed Max out of the room. 'This boy notices the right things' he thought.

Chapter 32

Gerry knew it would be at least ten hours before the doors opened again. He tried to sleep but only managed fitful moments. Each time he started to drop off he would wake up with a start, remembering the woman. His heart was racing. The thought of there being another human being within only a few yards of him was electric. He was beginning to get used to not being in control of his thoughts but it scared him.

His mind kept playing imaginary scenarios of how they communicate. Though rationally he knew it was very likely they would have great difficulty doing so. And, of course, she might not be a 'specimen' like him. She might actually be there to observe him! By 3 am sleep had finally relieved his tormented mind.

The next morning he was awake early. He showered and ate breakfast in a hurry – he wanted to be sure to be ready when the doors opened. Then he positioned is chair for maximum view and sat down with his paper and pencil. He did his routine chores with his lists and marked off the day. It was Sunday.

Finally at 9 am the door opened. The door of the newcomer's cell was already open, and the woman was standing in the window looking at him. He could only imagine what thoughts had been going through her head. At first they just stared at each other, each waiting for the other to make the first move. Then they both started to move slightly and suddenly there was an avalanche of movement and they were soon waving at each other. Gerry was in tears, experiencing a cocktail of emotions that couldn't really be described and to which he was completely unused. He picked up his notepad and wrote simply 'Hello'.

She strained to read the small writing, but then laughed and nodded. Clearly she did not have any writing equipment – he didn't expect her to. So this was going to have to be a one sided conversation, with questions requiring yes or no answers. He was aware of the limited supply that he had of both pencil lead and paper. He communicated this to the woman. She understood.

Finally he wrote; I NEED TO WORK OUT A SYSTEM SO THAT WE CAN GO ON COMMUNICATING. She nodded her agreement and they gave each other a wave. It was one of the most emotional human encounters he had ever experienced.

Chapter 33

Over dinner, Max talked with three of the other students who had also been hand-picked to attend the weekend. They had similar backgrounds to his. They would become firm friends, a friendship that would have a significant affect not only on their lives, but also on the lives of millions of other people.

Carl had graduated in computer science at Cambridge, specialising in artificial intelligence. His family were Swiss and had a long pedigree of involvement in politics. He was tall and willowy and had a shy manner that was somehow expected of people in his discipline. No one there could have predicted the changes in his bearing or appearance that would accompany his ageing.

Aditya was a graduate in political theory, an Oxford graduate like Max. His home was in India. He lived up to his name by being outspoken and controversial. Despite his diminutive stature, he was wiry and very strong and had recourse to self-defensive techniques that would leave the occasional adversary, who resorted to physical expressions of their disagreement, temporarily paralysed.

Shou was from Peking. He had graduated in anthropology at Cambridge, having been attracted particularly by the scientific pedigree of Trinity College. He spoke immensely fast and with great accuracy. The speed of his delivery gave the impression of excessive enthusiasm, which at first Max found distinctly off-putting. He was convinced that he would never get on with Shou.

Their conversation over dinner and late into the night was at times heated and very energetic. Aditya was particularly interested in evolutionary theories of politics. Carl was unsurprisingly fascinated by the potential of Artificial Intelligence. He showed this fascination with a somewhat cheesy grin – when he wasn't being self-conscious. Shou was excited by the comparison of different cultures and the roots of their values.

100

Max was rather more pragmatic than his new friends and was interested in what could actually be done in practice.

"In my view," Aditya's bearing and expression revealed a humility that was not so easily perceived in his words, "political systems evolve - using the same principles as the evolution of living organisms. They serve a base and cruel master, which is the unconscious drive of genetic material to replicate itself. The political systems that fulfil that objective best will eventually dominate."

"Maybe, but the development of artificial entities with superior intelligence to humans will surely alter that course." Carl's eyes were half closed as his attention was focussed on a vision of the future.

Aditya had assumed his favourite position for thinking and studying – cross-legged on the floor. In this position he could be completely immune to the conversations going on around him. On the other hand, and somewhat unnervingly, he would suddenly emerge from his meditative state with a complete knowledge of all that had been going on. This was such an occasion.

"I agree Carl – but although in the old days humans used to program computers, the new generation teach and program themselves. We might not be able to predict, or even know what they are doing in the future."

"Aditya – are you suggesting that machines will displace humans?"

"I don't think they can – if I'm right that it's our genes that govern what we do, they are hardly likely to lead to the evolution of machines that destroy them."

"Unless – ", Max had been chewing his toothpick for a while and saying nothing – "unless they develop their own equivalent of a genetic code, which turns out to be stronger, more dominant as it were."

Both the other young men nodded in agreement. Aditya gave a look as if to say 'why did I not think of that?' and retreated back into his own world.

"In which case what we need to do is control the way that artificial genetic code gets set up in the first place" Max concluded.

"But don't you think…"

Shou's eyes were bright and darted about the room from person to person. He seemed able to engage with all three of them simultaneously;

"don't you think the most important part of human evolution is conceptual? I mean, it's our value systems that define how we respond to our instincts?"

He retained Carl's gaze longer than the others. His comments had triggered off a chain of creative thoughts.

They would not remember the four exquisite courses, or the wine that would have sold for a week's salary per bottle. They would not have noticed that their every word was being monitored in another room in the hotel. What they would remember was that they started to evolve a vision of the world's future politics. They had, however, absolutely no reason to believe they would be instrumental in bringing that vision to reality; no more than any other group of slightly drunk people solving the world's problems in a late night discussion.

Chapter 34

Avril's fridge was fully stocked and she noticed that some items had not been there the day before. She had no recollection of hearing any operatives coming into her apartment. She shrugged her eyebrows. She was still wondering about the food as she returned to her living room. She noticed Gerry's doors opening. She was puzzled about the lack of information from the authorities though. No briefing, no 'job description' and apparently no way to get to the only other human in range.

The man was gesticulating – clearly trying to gain her attention. She was more than happy to oblige, although she had been a bit concerned by his behaviour the day before. He had seemed a bit desperate. He had written a new message on a piece of paper. Avril thought his use of such an outdated medium quite resourceful but, there again, what sort of person would have paper and pencil these days? They were museum items. His new message was quite short;

"Do you know sign language?"

She shook her head and laughed. Why would she? To her surprise, the man looked severely disappointed. Unconsciously she made a gesture that implied 'what's the matter?' Clearly he understood that and replied;

"I'm going to teach you some basic signs."

She replied with a thumbs up. She thought it would help pass the time of day, although she didn't approach the topic with the same urgency that Gerry did. They spent the first lesson rehearsing the alphabet. Gerry planned to build on the obvious foundation with a small selection of words that they would need to use frequently. But first he wanted to know what the woman was doing in a zoo enclosure.

"Do you know why you are here?"

She didn't need to sign the reply to that. She just shook her head. She signed "do you?"

"I think I'm a kind of zoo specimen! I used to be a scientist working here. But now I'm a caged animal. I've been demoted to 'retained'. No one has explained why."

"Same here" she replied but with humour. "When do you think we'll find out what's going on?"

"I don't think we will."

He left the stark words hanging. Avril felt a shiver down her back as it gradually dawned on her that he was being quite serious.

"Are you serious?"

She seemed to peer deeply into Gerry's eyes. Had he been closer he would have noticed that her pupils were heavily diluted. Then tears began to form.

"Do you think I am a zoo animal too?"

"I'm afraid I do."

Chapter 35

The rest of the weekend was a whirlwind of meetings and discussion groups. There were a handful of other graduates present and a sprinkling of leaders - mysterious and clearly powerful men who ran the conference. All the discussions were about politics and technological developments. The graduates were invited to air their views and although the leaders engaged actively in discussions they didn't reveal much of their own views.

What Max noticed about all of them was their ability to understand extensive technical detail but also get the big picture. What Max also noticed was that still no one had explained who was running this show or exactly what the purpose was. At the end of the sessions on the Saturday there was a plenary. Simon Barrington took the chair.

"Any questions?"

He wore a barely disguised quizzical grin. He knew what was coming and by now he pretty much knew who was going to ask the question. Aditya spoke up. He didn't raise his hand and if he felt any sense of apprehension he didn't show it. He seemed to be entirely unfazed by strangers of any status of level of intelligence.

"Two questions; who *are* you? And, why are we here?"

"Good questions – anyone care to hazard a guess?"

One of the other graduates spoke.

"We presume you're spooks, recruiting for MI5, 6 or GCHQ."

Simon exchanged a conspiratorial grin with Major General Sir David Carsons. David rose to field the question.

"Well no, actually, although I can see why you might think that. Simon does in fact work at GCHQ, I'm in the army..." - he didn't reveal his lofty rank - "and the rest can tell you who they are themselves. Sorry to say we're not recruiting and actually we don't belong to any organisation as such."

"So what is the strange masonic logo all about?"

Max thought he'd have a go at the direct approach.

"Ah, yes, the logo. Difficult to explain. All the people you see here share certain values and concerns. We hope that some of you may do too. You're here for us to find out – and thank you all for being so cooperative – so far!"

A small ripple of laughter went around the room.

"As you've probably noticed, you haven't been asked to sign the official secrets act or give any other similar undertaking and you won't be contacted directly by any of us again. At worst you will have had an enjoyable and very expensive weekend holiday at no cost to you. At best you may have learnt some useful things and made some useful contacts."

Since David's answer had produced more confusion than enlightenment but also made it clear there was no further information to be obtained, the questions dried up pretty quickly. At dinner the leaders were all absent, which allowed the participants to speak freely.

For a while a group of the guests simply talked about the events of the day. In addition to Max, Carl, Shou and Aditya there were two other guests: Marcus and Andrea. They also were high-fliers academically; Marcus had a degree in statistics and Andrea one in Genetics. Once the main course had been served the table staff disappeared and the young people were left alone. Max launched into a new topic.

"So, why do we think we are all here then? Marcus – you're the statistician – what's the probability of a mix like us being got together?"

Marcus was heavily involved in the process of getting a mouthful of the choice welsh lamb into his mouth. Clearly multi-tasking was not high in his skill set. After a while he transferred his attention to Max's question.

"I think the probability is very high – indeed a hundred percent."

"How do you work that out?" The others were all amused.

"I believe that whoever this organisation is, it has set out to find some high achieving graduates in politics, computer science, statistics and genetics. Given that there are plenty of potential candidates around, the probability of their being successful would be very high. They could hardly fail!"

He wore a slight grin as he was making a bit of a joke at the others' expense. Andrea alone seemed to get the joke. She gave a little chuckle.

"I think that if you wanted to get together a group of people who would have the technical knowledge and expertise to try to predict major global changes you would probably pick a bunch like us – though why you would choose to have two politicians is beyond me."

"Or an anthropologist!" – Shou was making fun of himself.

Max smiled benignly. Marcus commented;

"It seems odd that only two of us come from outside Europe. My money would be on Aditya being here for his cultural background more than his knowledge of politics. But Shou… why are you here?"

Aditya looked up briefly at the mention of his name but seeing that his contribution was not required returned to his own thoughts. Shou merely opened his hands as if to say 'don't ask me'. Marcus' comment, though completely ignored at the time, would prove to have been prophetic.

"But who are these people?" Aditya seemed keen to take the attention away from himself, his gaze remaining fixed on the distant location of his thoughts.

Andrea had been trying to release a tiny piece of meat that had rooted itself between two of her teeth. She poised, with the tooth-pick half elevated;

"Well, assuming they are telling the truth, we know they're not in the security services and none of us has recognised any of them as being politicians, so they're either a bunch of time-wasting weirdos – or…"

Her words trailed off as she seemed unable to frame the alternative. Max filled in for her. He leant forward with a strangely animated look on his normally rather dull face.

"Or they are part of a group of very powerful and influential people. They seem to have access to some very expensive resources. I mean, how did you all get involved first?"

The group rehearsed their first meetings, their strange encounters with people at University career fayres, being entertained at a very exclusive London club. They had all come by the same route and clearly the mysterious people who had brought them to this weekend had access to confidential and privileged information about all the guests.

"Clearly we're being selected for something!" observed Carl. They all agreed. "But the thing is we don't know what for!" He had been scratching his head but the itch had clearly disappeared some time ago, leaving his hand pointlessly hovering over his full head of ginger hair.

The weekend officially finished after Sunday lunch. There were no formal sessions in the morning but various discussion groups formed amongst the participants. As Max was leaving the house Shou rushed up to him and grabbed him by the arm.

"We must speak further – and with Carl. Can we meet sometime?"

Max hadn't given much thought to meeting up with any of them and he certainly hadn't planned to add Shou to his Christmas card list. But something in the man's intense look made Max think again.

The leaders weren't seen again and the candidates left with a strong desire to remain in contact but an overall sense of disappointment. There was no paperwork, no handouts, no business cards – in fact whatever this organisation was, it seemed determined keep any light it had firmly covered by its bushel.

Chapter 36

Max was reflecting on this strange meeting as Gabriel drove him to his appointment. His encounter with David, Simon and the other mysterious but clearly influential men had not led directly to a job, as indeed they had said it wouldn't. But he had found a number of doors opened very easily for him. He had applied for a role in the Civil Service and breezed into it. His promotions had come quickly and by the time he was fifty years old he was Director of the IDIC in Zurich.

Max had kept up contact with Carl and recovered his old friendship with Aditya after a period of separation enforced by circumstances; both men coincidentally had experienced similarly meteoric rises in their careers. They would occasionally comment humorously on the 'hand of fate' being upon them. Max would remind them that that phrase had an unfortunate history.

The International Directorate for Information Control managed the infrastructure for the Hub. It wasn't a purpose built system. Rather it combined the vast array of intelligent devices that had already existed before the demise of the World Wide Web.

The web had failed for a number of reasons, not least its essentially anonymous nature. The result of that was that it proved impossible to police. It therefore became the natural home for high value criminals, drug and people traffickers and terrorists. Its successor had political control built into it. The Hub was initially designed to be a universal search system, principally with policing and anti-terrorist objectives in mind.

The new 'web' replaced the protocols of the old whilst retaining all the means of connection – telecommunication wires, optic fibre cables and satellite links. Since all the devices coming under the umbrella title 'internet of things', along with most security devices like surveillance cameras and access controls, were all connected to the new web, the role of the Hub was subtly increased until it became what, in a former age, might have been called 'big brother'.

Carl and Max were to be the effective architects of this new system and the Prime Directives, which controlled the Hub's activity, were the result of their passionate desire to preserve what was left of the world's genetic variety. They happened to be in the right place at the right time to surf the wave of conservatism that followed a nuclear war. For this reason, and perhaps for the reasons alluded to by their mysterious hosts at the Old Rectory, political doors were opened to them. When Max was first invited to become a member of the Zurich group the final piece of his power jigsaw fell into place. He was, by then, a man of considerable experience in international diplomacy, and fortunately a person of impeccable morals and integrity.

Gabriel was navigating the streets with consummate ease. Max was on his way to meet his old friend Aditya, now the head of the Indian Civil Services. Their rendezvous was to be a rented office in a suite in central Delhi. They would enter by different doors, off different streets, at different times and collect their key passes from two shadowy characters each individually known to their mark but unknown to each other. Half an hour previous to Max's arrival there had been a small but very loud disturbance in the next street which had attracted the attention of the public and the police. Their carefully staged meeting used one of several dozen different templates, the identity of which was only revealed a few hours before their meetings, and communicated via the secret Vector channel.

Aditya was one of a number of Max's 'off-grid' contacts – people in the so-called East. IDIC didn't officially endorse his making these contacts but it realised that information needed to be gathered from, and sometimes released to, key people in the East. As the Director of IDIC, Max had free reign to talk to whomever he wished. Aditya had already been briefed by Max about the state of affairs in the West and had been alerted to the potential danger of the Hub putting his and millions of other people's lives at risk. Max wanted to bring him up to speed and talk over the detail of the proposed changes to the prime directives that could sign or rescind the death warrants of the vast majority of the world's population.

This kind of thing could not be done on Vector. You had to see the other person's eyes, detect their emotions, gauge their honesty – do a hundred and one things that are communicated visually; and even a video link couldn't do all that. In any case, Max enjoyed meeting his old friend. They had known each other for over thirty years. He hoped they would continue to be able to be friends for another thirty.

Chapter 37

Avril was amazed at the speed with which she became quite fluent in using signs. As their visual vocabulary increased, the chimp opposite Gerry began to take more interest in Gerry's movements; but it was clearly only a superficial interest. Gerry was relieved to have found a faster learner. They spent some time sharing experiences of the past few days, comparing their living conditions and trying to work out why they were incarcerated in a zoo. Eventually they lost focus and started to quiz each other about their lives. Finally, when Avril described recognising her own ID in one of her demotions, Gerry began to take notice.

"What document did you say it was?"

"A demotion – there were two actually, the same week. Both ordinary operatives being demoted to 'retained'."

"How many?!"

"Two – oh! – oh, my God – you don't think you were the other one?!"

There was no real reason to suspect such a coincidence. The Hub processed millions of court orders daily. Jobs like Avril's were parcelled out randomly to thousands of legal operatives. The two she had dealt with could have related to people thousands of miles away. But she had been shocked by the demotion of a valid human and maybe that had predisposed her to drawing the inference.

The documents in question had only referred to the operatives by their ID; but for her aunt's name she wouldn't have recognised her own – very few people bothered to memorise their own 24 character ID. Your PIDAC remembered it for you. And she certainly hadn't memorised either of the two she had processed that day.

"Did the document say any more about your status?"

"No."

"What about the other one?"

"It said it was 'research subject'."

"Did it say why?"

"Rare genetic material – Species Hs53."

Gerry knew about Hs53. He knew it referred to an extinct branch of human evolution that was thought to be genetically isolated from modern *Homo sapiens*. That is, until DNA analysis had shown that at least one living human being contained fragments of Hs53's DNA. The search was on then for other matches. In the previous six months the Hub had identified only four likely matches in the whole population of the West. Now it dawned on him that he was probably one of the four. He imparted this knowledge to Avril. Their arms were still for several minutes as both took in the significance of their discovery.

"But what about you? What was the reason for your demotion?"

"I can't remember what it said – lots of technical references."

"Can you recall anything at all?"

"Something about a 'superfamily'."

"O.R. superfamily?"

"Yes – that was it. Hyper-something. What does that mean?"

"Hyperosmia; it means you've got an enhanced sense of smell!"

"That's true. But why would that make them put me in here?"

"Well it's linked to an ancient gene sequence."

"Like you!"

"Yes – now we know why we've both ended up here."

"With the chimps!"

Although the revelation was not encouraging, it did at least explain their situation. For a moment they were both lost in their own thoughts, yet their eyes remained locked on each other.

Chapter 38

Entering the south foyer, Max was checked for bugs. It was one of the routine services offered by this facility. Max entered the room first, took a seat at the desk looking out over the street. The room was on the 12th floor and the office block had tinted windows. There was no chance of anyone seeing in. The desk was clear. There were no signs of any comms device anywhere and Max's advance team had swept the office for bugs. Max did not have anything with him – no Holoviewer, not even a simple mobile comms unit.

Presently the door opened and Aditya entered. Both men were silent until the door was shut. Then they embraced one another. It had been several months since their previous meeting. Aditya sat beside Max at a 45 degree angle, both looking out of the window.

"The Prime Directives."

Aditya's statement was an invitation to Max to start.

"Yes, the very first in fact."

Aditya raised his eyebrows.

"The one that protects the lives of *Homo sapiens*."

"Almost."

"Well, yes, I know – valid humans."

Aditya registered a wry smile, exposing a set of rather yellow teeth.

He was well used to the neo-fascism of the Hub but it didn't really trouble him. He'd rather live in the so-called East any day. It had real people, living real lives, making real choices, having real freedom. In any case he knew that true freedom derived from having a well-disciplined mind. Max cast a glance in

Aditya's direction but studiously avoided any emotional response to the remark. He understood Aditya's position, though he didn't see things that way.

"Well, there is a proposal to change it slightly, since we perceive a danger that the Hub may react aggressively to the East's increasing social unrest."

What an understatement, both men thought. Aditya knew about the danger. This was going to be the first time he had been given any detail about the solution.

"Until now, the East has benefitted from the fact that we depend on it for a large number of resources. But with the diminution of that trade and the increasing unrest in your sector, there is a chance that the Hub will implement model 5."

Aditya nodded. He knew about model 5 too – Max had told him.

"PD 247 protects valid humans with ancient EGSs - extinct gene sequences. That excludes deacts and of course anyone who is outside the Hub."

"That would be about six billion people?"

"Yes about that – haven't counted recently!"

"Neither have we!"

The men exchanged a slight smile. Despite the fact they represented two enormous populations which were in direct competition with other, one of which had the ability to completely wipe out the other, the men were not enemies. They understood the need to preserve diversity. Evolution depended on it.

"So, we are working on bringing humans in the East under the protection of PD 247. The Hub will know that there is a significant statistical probability that East humans contain samples of such genetic material and this alteration should ensure the security of your people."

"Have you run tests?"

"Only small scale. The Hub works with two billion human operatives and in excess of a thousand billion connected intelligent devices. The only way you could model that much data would be by running the test live."

Aditya raised his eyebrows again. He knew this really but he thought it was worth asking.

"The thing is, it's not just a matter of changing some words in a sentence."

"Of course not. The directives are human readable sentences that get converted into hundreds of classifier rules."

"Quite. Our chaps are working on it now. What we need, that we don't currently have, is a list of the EGSs that have been found in your laboratories. Our guess is that they may contain some different strains from ours which would strengthen your protection."

"I'm not sure I understand – why not just make a few up!"

"We're going to need some actual samples that can be analysed by our system. The Hub would treat any hear-say references as an attempt at espionage, which would undermine everything."

"Of course."

The two men talked on about the number of samples that might be needed and the diplomatic problem of getting them into the West without detection.

"How long do you think it might take to find some samples?"

"Hopefully less than six months."

"Hm, I think we need to be a bit quicker."

"Why?"

"Well our simulation of the deterioration of the present situation suggests it might go critical within three weeks."

"Goodness!"

Aditya thought for a moment. His highly disciplined mind having concluded whatever business it had been about, his presence returned to the room.

"We'll see what can be done Max."

The two men stood and shook hands. Aditya left first. Ten minutes later Max left and took a different route.

The plan was in play.

Chapter 39

Max met Carl at Glanzenberg. It wasn't a formal meeting of the Zurich group but then no meeting of the Zurich group was formal. However, usually all members were advised of a forthcoming meeting and could attend it if they wished. This one had not been advertised. Accordingly they had the run of the building – but on the down side there was no tea and cake.

For no particular reason the two men gravitated towards the room with the dining table. They turned two chairs towards one another and each sat with one elbow on the table, like gentlemen after dinner. If the business of the Zurich group was off-record, this meeting was off-off-record. Some members of the Zurich group knew about the proposed change to PD 247, but no one apart from Carl knew about Max's visit to India. The three friends who had met all those years ago at a country Manor hotel had retained an absolute trust in, and loyalty to, one another.

"How soon can they get us some samples?"

"Hopefully three weeks…"

"I hope so too. The signs aren't good."

"How's the coding going?"

Max was sitting upright on a none-too comfortable dining chair. His powers of concentration meant that he was oblivious to discomfort. He looked Carl straight in the eye.

"Strictly speaking it's not coding Max." Carl was looking through one open eye, the other one tight shut indicating concentration, or at least giving the semblance of it. Carl was an expert poker player. "We're working on the classifier rules and building in some place-holders until you can provide us with some data that the Hub will no doubt find once we've put it somewhere not too obvious!"

"How are you going to do that?"

"There are some archive files relating to research cooperation between our universities and those of the East. The files pre-date the creation of the Hub. There are change monitors on all archive repositories, so we can't simply call them up on-screen and type something new. We are going to have to create a maintenance program for the hardware and slip in the new data when the hardware is officially off-line."

"So you'll be re-writing history!"

"Just a little." Carl allowed himself a little grin.

"Brilliant – what fun." Max's face was dead pan. He would often engage in little linguistic games without really thinking about it. It helped to confuse eaves-droppers. "Any chance of being noticed?"

"Yes – every chance. Archive repositories are kept under the highest security. But I'm sure we can manage it."

"And then, how do you get the actual sample into the WGB sample store?"

"Oddly enough that's easier. There is a regular maintenance protocol. The air conditioning units have to be updated *before* they ever go wrong, so parts are replaced before half of their expected life time. That means there are frequent maintenance cycles and engineers have to enter the stores with boxes of tools and parts – not to mention sandwiches! Popping a few test tubes into a couple of empty slots should be a doddle."

"Won't the Hub notice that occupancy has changed?"

"No, there's a flaw in the system there. When the stores were set up it was assumed that no one would ever be tempted to alter the number of archived units. They just didn't think of it. They were thinking about scientists – not political espionage agents!"

"Is that what we are?" He offered this remark without any obvious sense of interest.

"No, Max, we're the saviours of mankind. That's what we are!" He fixed Max with a long stare that hinted at the depth of their friendship.

At least one member of the group had a different view of Max.

Chapter 40

Gerry had spent the next night trying to rack his brains. He remembered the olfactory impact of Avril's unique gene sequence but he was sure there was something else. His problem was that, although he had been reading about the technical details only a day or so before he lost his freedom, there was a host of references and associated consequences associated with differing gene sequences. He just couldn't remember which went with which. He remembered that his own unique genetic remnant, Hs53, was thought to produce an increased tolerance to radiation. But he was pretty sure there was no connection with an increased sense of smell. He was suspicious as to why two human samples had been placed in the same zoo at about the same time. From a researcher's point of view this looked like part of a plan. Maybe smell was what it was, though he couldn't think of a reason for researching it. But then that was the superior mental strength of the Hub. It had access to a level of intelligence, albeit artificial, that far out-stripped his or any other human's intelligence. If the Hub was onto something there would be no more reason to expect to know what it was onto than to expect to understand the mind of the almighty! A whole list of possible effects of Hs53, beneficial and otherwise, cluttered his tired mind.

Avril's mind was equally worried but with different thoughts. Emotionally she was a day or so behind Gerry, since she had only recently understood the severity of her situation. She was thinking about her mother and what the authorities would have told her about her daughter. Since Avril couldn't know what they would have told her, in fact, her imagination was free to dream up a whole list of worse-case scenarios. Her normal happy fatalism had given way to a sense of apprehension that was as frightening an experience as it was fresh.

Her historic genetic background was of no interest to her. She had always had a ridiculously keen sense of smell. It was annoying, mostly, and brought little in the way of advantage in life – except perhaps getting her that lab assistant's job in the sixth form!

As a distraction she tried to rehearse the words and phrases she had learnt in their sign-language session. As she practised various signs in front of the mirror she caught sight of herself and for a moment allowed herself a little humour. As she was practising an operative came silently into the room. It was the early evening routine. Emptying trash, cleaning the floor, re-stocking the fridge. It was so routine that Avril barely noticed it was there - until, without warning, it suddenly did something completely unexpected, and Avril knew immediately that her relationship with her new found friend and ally was probably over.

Chapter 41

Aditya had left his meeting with Max thinking about the enormity of the task that lay ahead of him.

When the last gasps of diplomacy had given up the ghost, fifty years before, the world had descended into chaos. The middle east, as predicted, was the focus of a third world war and as the throttle-hold of the Arab states over fuel supplies was weakened by the development of hydrogen technologies, an unholy alliance of mostly western powers had decided to wipe the slate clean. Israel, Palestine and most of the states around the Persian Gulf were flattened and nuclear weapons that had lain untested and unused finally got their brief moment. Their makers were rewarded with an avalanche of 'test' results.

A huge swathe of land, from and including Georgia in the north through to Egypt in the West, Yemen in the South and Iran in the East, became an irradiated no-man's land. Many of the remaining oil-wells, now uncontrolled, became permanent beacons of thick black smoke. The principle advantage from the Western powers' point of view was that it had a new thousand mile boundary that would not need policing for several millennia. Satellite-born lasers monitored the border with Russia and with the threat of a massive store of nuclear missiles aimed at Russia, all was quiet on the Eastern front! That left a mixed bag of Eastern nations which were deprived of connections with the West and outside of the benefits of the new technological revolution.

Aditya had in effect been marooned behind the new wall. It was to take him several years to find a way of getting in touch with his old friends Max and Carl. They never quite understood what had been happening at the weekend they spent at the country manor but the strength and resilience of their relationship kept them seeking one another's contact like parted lovers.

Chapter 42

It was a nondescript Tuesday when Aditya made a life-changing decision to try to find Max. He had been thinking about him off and on for years. But, ever the since the final separation of East and West by the western powers' adoption of the Hub and all its intricate technologies, he had consigned the plan to find Max to the back his mind.

On the previous night he had had a strange dream. They were back at the weekend conference where they had first met and they had been walking in the grounds of the house. Suddenly Max fell into the lake and Aditya was torn between jumping in to save his friend, or staying on the side and saving his own life. He awoke in a sweat with a strong compunction to resolve the tension which had been surfaced by the dream.

His last contact with Max had been before the outbreak of war nearly three decades before. They had met at a political conference in Geneva. It had focused on the possible change in middle-east politics which was predicted to occur as a result of the development of hydrogen fuel technologies.

Quite unexpectedly diplomatic relations between a whole raft of nations had rapidly broken down and communications between India and Britain had soon become all but impossible. The government department for which Aditya was then working refocused its attention on countries to its East and Max became increasingly occupied with relations between Britain and the US.

On this fateful Tuesday morning Aditya decided it was time to find Max. However, he hadn't the faintest idea how he was going to do it.

That same morning Max arose late, having celebrated a minor birthday the day before. He was due to meet the US ambassador that afternoon and he needed to re-hydrate his head. The

126

ambassador was John Gilbert, a republican by inheritance, but with little in the way of an interest in old fashioned politics. He and Max had met at a drinks party and hit it off immediately, ending their first conversation at 1am after being exclusively involved with one another for four hours. John was tall, thin and bald. A great team leader – not least because you could always pick him out in a crowd.

He had recently been appointed as ambassador to India and was keen to take soundings from Max. Like many enlightened people at the time, they could see that the splitting of the world into two politically separate zones was merely an investment in a future calamity. John had frequently voiced his concerns to Max and they had come to the conclusion there would need to be a form of unofficial channel of communication between the two – a form of 'back door' into each other's information back-bone.

Max, it would transpire, would be in an ideal position to make this happen, when he became leader of IDIC. They met for lunch and John opened up.

"Max – so good to see you!"

They exchanged a lingering hug.

"When are you going to Delhi?"

"Oh I'm not. These days we don't send people to the East. We just use video links. Communication is closely controlled."

"I knew that was the case for mere mortals such as myself - but I would have thought that people in your position would need to have a physical presence."

"Oh well, diplomacy isn't what it used to be."

They both laughed at the joke as Max poured the wine."

"It's a pity though – there was someone I was hoping you might be able to trace for me."

"I can try – who is it?"

"Aditya Ghatak – he's a rising star in the Indian Civil Service."

"You can say that again! We think he will go right to the top."

"You know him?"

"Of him, certainly. But I don't have the clearance to talk to him directly. Why do you want to talk to him?"

"Oh, we were good friends for years, but we lost contact."

The two men were silent as they reflected on the long list of close international friendships that had been broken by the drifting of the political plates on which they found themselves increasingly marooned.

"Between you and me Max, I think it would be a very good idea for you two to get in touch again. But also a good idea to keep your relationship quiet."

"Interesting – why?" Max looked at him with a blankness that spoke more of innocence than anything else. It was a practised look which Max had found to be very effective in elucidating information from unwilling informants. By now it had become second nature.

"I think he could be well placed to form a foundation for our communication 'back door'. As it happens, I have a budget and some latitude for developing alternative diplomatic avenues. If you and Aditya can work out something that won't cost an arm and a leg, we might hide it in my budget."

Within a month the two old friends had been reunited and the foundation on which 'Vector' would later be built was laid. Max's dream became a reality. Aditya's was never mentioned.

While the West had adapted the burgeoning new technology to provide a universal monitoring system - the Hub - the East relied on a technical network that was a century out of date.

When Aditya and Max had finally made contact, they found that their political positions had parted considerably. Max, as one of the architects of the new system, was happy with the loss of private privilege that it entailed. He only had to recall images of the war to remember why this sort of control was necessary.

Aditya conversely only had to recall the horror stories of his and other families' experience of being near the war zone to realise that technology had done this and they were better off with less of it. But he never for a moment thought of Max as an enemy. Max was a product of his world just as Aditya was of his own. And their passionate objective was still as it had always been; to find some way to enable eight billion people to co-exist on the one planet. To preserve what was left of other species and the genetic heritage was a secondary objective for Aditya, but an equal primary one for Max.

So when Max had proposed meeting him and briefing him about the workings of the Hub, and the need for a secret channel of communication, he was only too pleased to agree. They used John Gilbert's funds to set up a secret meeting in Switzerland, where Max had recently been invited to join a rather shadowy group of highly influential people. That discussion led him to become probably the most privileged person in the East in terms of knowledge. And the secrecy that their initial meeting had instilled in them ensured that it remained that way.

So now his task was to secretly discover minute samples of pre-historic genetic material in a couple of continents where communication was rudimentary and fear and suspicion were rife. It was true he only needed half a dozen but it was still like looking for a needle in a pile of a thousand haystacks. Of course he couldn't do this on his own. He needed someone in the right place, with the right expertise and whom he could trust absolutely. There was one person – and that was Mukti.

Chapter 43

Avril had realised that she hadn't given the man her name. Nor did she know his. So, by way of practice, she had been signing her name in the mirror. She was doing this when she saw the operative come into the room behind her. She saw it clearly in the mirror and as she finished signing "m y n a m e i s a v r i l" the operative suddenly spoke;

"Hello Avril. How can I help you?"

That was the moment she realised that her discussions with the man were doomed. If the operatives could read their sign language – and even when reversed in the mirror – then the other observation cameras in the rooms must be able to as well. Did the man realise this? Presumably not otherwise he would have been more cautious. She spent a fitful night, perpetually waking in a sweat and trying desperately to think of a way around the problem. She thought it was unlikely that the Hub had already monitored their conversations because surely it would have done something already. There again, there wasn't anything particularly significant in what they had said so far, so maybe it had just dismissed their messages as irrelevant. But irrelevant to what? This just brought her back to question 'what are we here for?'

The next day, she decided not to go to the window until she had thought up a strategy. She needed to take over the conversation and alert him – but not in a way that might alert the Hub. She thought a straightforward description of the event might be the simplest. Soon the man appeared – he had probably been coming back every few minutes to check if she were there. Avril signalled a greeting.

"Hi"

"Hi. How did you sleep?"

"Oh fine," she lied.

Gerry could tell from her demeanor that something was wrong.

"Are you sure? You look worried."

"No I'm fine. It's funny actually. "Last night I was practising my signing in the mirror when an operative came in and answered me back."

As she anticipated, this news had a dramatic effect on the man. He put his finger to his mouth and pursed his lips, no doubt miming 'shhh'.

Then he walked away from the window. Gerry retreated to his kitchen and sat on a stool by the bar. The same thoughts that had gone through Avril's mind now went through his. His mind flipped back to problem solving. That was what he enjoyed most. He would lose himself in entertaining a multiplicity of possible explanations and in trying to weigh the competing arguments. Complex thinking had always been his means of distraction.

He wondered if there was some way to hijack an operative and get a message to the girl. Perhaps there is a crack in the operative's outer covering into which he could slip a note. Surely not everything is monitored? But there would be no guarantee that the same operative was servicing both rooms. And how could he indicate to her that this was his plan? And how could she reply – there would be no chance of hiding a pencil in his Trojan operative! The alternative was to carry on as normal but be careful what they said. Difficult – he had no idea what they were going to say and in any case they needed to act as a team if they were going to find a way of getting out. This new danger had challenged Gerry to actually think of escaping. Up until now he had been obsessed with trying to work out why they were there.

A plan began to hatch in his mind. If they were going to defeat their automaton jailers it would have to be done by bluff. For all the super intelligence of the Hub and its network of artificial geniuses, it had not had to contend with a great deal of deceit. Humans had become very compliant in their comfortable, organised world. Consequently the Hub had not had much experience of deviousness. That was it – they would bluff their way out!

Chapter 44

Aditya and Mukti had met some ten years previously. They had been work colleagues when Aditya was working in the Ministry for External Affairs. They would socialise after work and talk politics. Aditya had a near perfect memory. He could scan a complex document and retain just about everything he had seen. And he was generous in his explanation of any topic in which anyone else showed the slightest interest. To many people this was both intimidating and boring, but for Mukti it was the root of a powerful attraction. A strong bond had grown and they had maintained their friendship, even when he was promoted and she moved to the Ministry of Home Affairs.

One of her tasks in that department had been the oversight of genetic research – considered to be a security issue as well as a scientific one. The role brought her into contact with a range of universities as well as government and commercial research departments.

At some point along the line Mukti had married and it became difficult for them to meet or talk any more. They would meet at the occasional conference and they would manage one or two telephone conversations each year.

The gravity of Aditya's present task emboldened him to make an unexpected contact. He decided not to telephone as many phone lines were bugged. He couldn't go to the house without raising her husband's suspicions, so he decided to go to her place of work and wait for her there.

Mukti was easily recognisable as she was unusually tall. As she walked around the corner of the main desk in her office building, Aditya rose from his seat and presented himself. She was visibly shocked and her voice betrayed her anxiety.

"Aditya! – what is it? Why have you come here?"

"I need to talk with you Mukti – something of the greatest importance and urgency."

The entrance lobby was a busy and noisy place and there was no fear of them being overheard. However, one of Mukti's colleagues might well see them and wonder what was going on. Aditya couldn't risk that.

"Please give me a room number where we can meet in ten minutes."

Mutki hesitated then quietly said "two three five, second floor. Don't knock, just walk in."

Mutki's work for the Ministry of Home Affairs often involved meeting people with questionable backgrounds. She would never have thought of the most senior civil servant as falling into that category. Ten minutes later, to the minute, Aditya opened the door of room 235, walked in and closed it quietly behind him. Mutki was sitting at a desk with her back to the door. The sun was pouring into the room across the desk but Mutki's face was in the shade. She knew how to be careful. She motioned to Aditya to take the chair in the shade.

"What can I do for you?"

Chapter 45

Carl sat in his usual seat in the conference room at Glanzenberg castle. He was biting his right thumb-nail – a sure sign of high stress levels. His normal ebullient self-confidence was absent. He was not in control of his destiny for a moment and that rattled him. Vector would not work outside the West. But he needed it. In ten minutes two members of the Zurich group would arrive for a meeting that one of them had requested. Max was unobtainable. He was on his way back from India.

His predicted absence had seemed to make the demand for a meeting all the more vociferous. Carl had stalled them when they requested information about Max's current location. Carl hadn't a clue about what they wanted but he desperately needed to know from Max whether there was anything he needed to know!

The other members of the group who were, at this moment, on the last lap of their journey from the airport, were Jacques Barre – the French PM – who knew about the proposed changes to PD 247; and Andrew Barrington – second in command of MI6 – who did not. Andrew was an infrequent visitor to the Castle. Max, of course, had met his father, for a brief weekend. That encounter, however, had not been long or deep enough to make Carl trust Simon so there was no reason why he would automatically trust the son. Indeed, Max had reason to be distinctly suspicious of Andrew and that centred on another member of the group whom he had met at the Old Rectory: Shou, the anthropologist.

Chapter 46

Unknown to Max, Shou and Andrew had met some years before Andrew was admitted to the inner sanctum of the Zurich group. Shou had previously suggested that Max, Atikya and he should get together, which indeed they did. It was not a very successful meeting. Max had not anticipated it would be. He had taken an instant dislike to Shou the first time they met and nothing that Shou said or did at their subsequent meet made Max feel any differently about him.

Max asked himself whether that was just prejudice. He concluded that it might well be, but he couldn't seem to do anything about it. On the other hand, it might just as well have been political. Max was a post-capitalist, he believed firmly in the possibility of techno-utopianism. Shou didn't. Shou realised all too clearly that for a technological solution to work in a population the size and poverty of China there would have to be a massive reduction in the size of that population.

Andrew had met Shou at an international conference and by chance had spent an evening in the bar. Somewhat surprisingly Max's name had cropped up.

"Oh, my father mentioned his name a few times. He thought very highly of Max – always said he could see him in a significant political role one day."

"I think that would be a bad idea."

Andrew was somewhat taken aback.

"Oh really? Why?"

"Well, Max has an altogether too high a level of confidence in humanity's ability to govern itself."

"What alternative is there?"

"Well the problem is that in capitalist and technology based cultures power is ultimately exercised by a ruling elite – to the severe detriment of the people."

Shou went on to elaborate his political thinking; and as the hours, and the drinks, went by he found himself agreeing more and more with Andrew, and less and less with his father. And therefore less with Max. The long-term effect of Shou's influence on Andrew was that Andrew had a deep-seated prejudice against Max which, coupled with his envy of the man who had taken the seat of power that he had always thought was rightfully his, led him to view Max as a potential traitor. When he had become head of MI6, he gained the perfect opportunity to put his prejudice in practice and he put a permanent tail on Max almost from the outset. Max's ability to evade surveillance only served to confirm Andrew's suspicion that Max was up to something.

Chapter 47

Andrew had been invited to join the Zurich group by the previous British PM, who had himself been a member for some time before he rose to that dizzy office. When Andrew had heard that Max was not going to attend, he suggested using the Hub personnel locator service. He could just as easily have used his own resources but he preferred not to use his precious budget unless he had to. This was temporarily to Carl's advantage.

The problem with using the Hub to find Max was that Max was currently in two places. In order for Max to be able to slip away unnoticed Carl had had a duplicate PIDAC made. This one was not implanted under Max's skin but kept in a lead-lined box. The device, being only a few millimetres in width, could be hidden in a cuff link box. PIDACs could not be turned off so, to prevent the Hub noticing a duplicate signal, Max would hide his second one away.

When he planned a secret mission he would meet Gabriel at a suitable and legitimate rendezvous. There the duplicate PIDAC would be removed from its shield and at the same time Max would put on an expensive scarf. It had been bought at Barney's in New York for the equivalent of a normal person's monthly salary. But what made it priceless was the microscopically thin, woven lead shield that it had been lined with.

The scarf effectively destroyed Max's implant's signal so the Hub now latched on to the duplicate. After a decent interval Gabriel would leave and take the duplicate back to Max's house. There it was attached to Max's dog's collar. The dog was old and frail and generally mooched about the house. Once a day the operative would come to clean and would walk the dog slowly. There was very little to alert the Hub to any highly unusual activity, so long as no one started looking for him.

A search would focus more of the Hub's computing power on the signals from Max's duplicate PIDAC and then alarm bells might ring. No, it was vital that no one searched for Max!

The concierge alerted Carl to the fact that Andrew had arrived. It would be only a few minutes now before he entered the room and started asking questions. Carl's Vector flashed. A single red light was repeating about once a second. He typed in his code – such old technology! The message that appeared on the screen was more effective in relaxing Carl's nerves than an hour's yoga;

"The dog collar is clean."

It was Max's code message to indicate that he was now back in the country and the dog was returned to its primary role of being singularly useless. The door opened suddenly and loudly, startling Carl.

Chapter 48

Andrew had been in his office, skimming over thousands of words, reports that he was supposed to be acquainted with. He was due to meet the Foreign Secretary and highlight the day's security issues. But all he could think of was Max. Andrew's tail had reported Max disappearing on a jet to India. What was he doing? Andrew also had several moles in IDIC and a message had come through that morning that caught his attention. It might not be a matter of national security but it was certainly of great importance to him personally – which, in Andrew's mind, somewhat unfortunately amounted to the same thing.

"William! What have you got for me?"

"Well this is strange. I've been monitoring comms here and I managed to get a peek into a conversation between Max Brunner and Carl Fische."

"How the hell did you manage that?"

"Let's say someone was careless. The Vector system is vulnerable when its users are careless."

"So what did you learn?"

"It seems they are planning a change to one of the PDs."

"The what?"

"Prime Directives – you know – the rules that control what the Hub can and can't do."

"What?! But they're fundamental. Change them and the whole course of history could be altered!"

"It seems that a change in the course of history is exactly what they have in mind."

"My God! Which one?"

"PD 247 – something to do with protecting species with unusual DNA or something."

Andrew spoke rapidly to his PA. "Put everything on hold 'til I get back."

"How long will you be?"

"I don't know."

She was unperturbed by Andrew's sudden change of plan. It wasn't unusual. His journey to Zurich was accompanied by a sense of trepidation. As it happens he had good reason to be worried.

Chapter 49

"So where is Max?" demanded Andrew, without bothering with a greeting.

"At home."

"Let me see."

Andrew took out his Vector and fiddled clumsily with the keypad. In a moment he had his answer. He snorted disapprovingly and put the device away. Carl, now very composed, resumed his disarming smile but spoke icily;

"Good morning Andrew. I hope you had a pleasant flight."

There was no reply. The concierge alerted Carl that Jacques was now on his way up. When the three men had sat down, Andrew opened the meeting.

"Tell me about PD 247."

That was it. No introduction, no briefing on events. Not even a question. Carl would not have expected Andrew to know anything about any of the directives by number. Detail was not his bag. So somebody somewhere must had said something. Carl replied by simply rehearsing the human definition. It was quite long and clearly did not contain the answer to Andrew's implied question.

"I don't want to know what it bloody means. I want to know why I am getting reports that the Hub has been running tests on a hypothetical situation involving a change to a PD!" By the end of the sentence he was shouting and he marked the final word with a thump on the table. "Does Max know about this?"

Carl replied in a measured tone. "I would not expect Max to know what Hub processes were being monitored by your lot."

"Dammit, you know that's not what I meant! Does Max know someone's experimenting with a change in a PD – you know, Prime Directive, the things that never get changed!"

So far, Andrew had been one of the many members of the Zurich group who were ignorant of the proposed changes to PD 247. Max was in charge of who knew and who didn't and Carl was not about to undermine that position.

"I really couldn't say, Andrew." Carl did his best to be opaque. Jacques took his lead from Carl and said nothing. It seemed to work for Andrew merely said;

"No one seems to know any bloody thing here these days. Sometimes I think it's a waste of my time."

At that moment Andrew's Vector lit up again. He read the message quickly.

"Ah – so something is up! Max wants us to meet him!"

What Andrew didn't know was that Carl had left his Vector on, relaying the conversation to Max. The meeting was scheduled for the next day, late afternoon. Andrew would have to find something to do for the rest of the day. There was plenty of opportunity.

Chapter 50

Aditya was uncharacteristically hesitant.

"How have you been? How are you?"

"Let's take it as read that we are both fine and so are our families. I have little time and yours must be very precious too. Please come to the point."

Aditya had forgotten how abrupt Mukti could be. A quality that had no doubt helped her exceptional rise in the civil service. But if you were on the receiving end of it, and you were uncertain of your position, she could be very intimidating.

"I have a very sensitive and vital request to make of you. The safety of billions of people may depend on the help that I hope you can give me."

Mukti looked concerned. She was trying to assess what sort of request could be made of her that had such truly awful consequences.

"I think I will need more information before I can give you an answer!"

"Of course. I merely wanted to underline how important an issue this is. I'm afraid I can't go into details that impinge on national security but I need to know if we can find six samples of this genetic variant amongst our population. Preferably from different races."

He slid a folded piece of paper across the desk. Mukti took it and opened it carefully. Her jaw dropped in amused amazement.

"You've come all this way to ask me to find a few genetic samples? You could have emailed me the request!"

The amusement faded from her face.

"I can't believe that you have wasted my time for this!"

"Yes I know it seems superficial. But for reasons I can't explain it is vital that no one knows about this."

There was a pause.

"I see. Well I suppose I shall have to take your word for that." said Mukti at length.

"I'm afraid you will."

"This will take me time – but it can be done, I'm sure. When do you want them by?"

"Three weeks at the latest."

"I'm finding it really difficult to take you seriously. Two months would be my best bet."

"Three weeks, absolute latest. There is no room for any kind of negotiation in this matter." He was staring her straight in the eyes. His initial diffidence had long been replaced by his natural confidence. There could be no doubt of the severity of the situation.

"Well, I will try. What do I get in return?"

He looked her in the eye again.

"If you're lucky – you get to live."

Chapter 51

The next morning Andrew left his hotel and went to the British Embassy. There he found a secure console and logged into his system. He had a short Videocon with his second-in-command. There was apparently some business that needed doing with a contact in Zurich. Andrew was not surprised. There usually was! He thought he would do a little skiing first. There would bound to be somewhere suitable within an hour's drive or so. His driver, a member of the cantonal police force, took him speedily to Einsiedeln, south of Zurich. He booked in and hired some skis and kit.

Andrew got into a lift and enjoyed watching the view open up before him. As he got out, he was pleased to see that there was no one else on the piste. The lift had been empty too. He had managed to give his bodyguard the slip in town! Andrew enjoyed his own company.

He had been skiing down the slope for only twenty or thirty seconds when a snow-boarder came from his right, at speed. It is doubtful that Andrew would have seen him coming. The board lifted off the snow and hit him with full force on the head. It was later reported as an unfortunate accident. It might have been fatal. The process of recovery was certainly going to keep Andrew occupied for several weeks. As one commentator put it, *the chances against it happening were immense. You couldn't have done it if you'd tried.* By this time Carl had returned home - and Max's trip to Zurich was cancelled.

Chapter 52

Gerry had been planning his strategy. The fact that the operative had responded to Avril's sign language was a surprise. It was a huge set-back in one way. But it made Gerry realise something which had just not occurred to him before. That he could communicate with the Hub. Since the day he had been imprisoned he had had no communication from the Hub except for it telling him the viewing door would be a day late opening.

However, now it appeared that it would communicate with the girl. That opened up all sorts of possibilities. Somehow he would try to get to the Hub through her. There was no doubt in his mind that the Hub was monitoring everything she said. Just as it monitored everything that everyone else ever said.

Chapter 53

Mutki was not impressed by her friend and former colleague's unannounced appearance. She wasn't entirely sure whether he was being truthful about the alleged consequences of her failing to deliver what he requested. She was annoyed to have had 30 minutes of her precious time wasted. She was irritated by now having the worry of whether someone might have noticed. Most of all she was angry that when she returned home, whatever her husband said, she would have a sense of guilt at having spent time with a former lover in secret. Almost certainly it would affect her demeanour. Almost certainly he would notice.

So now she had to waste even more time working out what she was going to say. She could hardly tell the truth! If Aditya was telling the truth, and was right about whatever it was that was worrying him so much, then it was paramount that she kept the confidence. Damn the man! Even more, she was incensed that he still could make her feel the way she was feeling now, even after all those years, and after all the things that he had done that made her realise he was not the demi-god she had first thought.

She slammed her car into third gear in order to get past some laggard in a rickshaw. That was her real mistake. The next thing she knew she was slamming on the brakes as a couple of children came out from behind the rickshaw. It was probably only a couple of *Dalits*. Probably no one would notice their demise. But in her position, she would be noticed, questions would be asked.

She pulled over and took out her mobile phone. She could have dialled 102 – the emergency ambulance service but the children would probably be dead before it arrived. Instead she dialled her own private hospital number. It was going to cost her a bit but it would be worth it for the PR value.

The ambulance arrived within a mere five minutes, such was the effect of the most expensive health plan that could be bought in

India. Close on its heels came a police car – not that anyone had called the police. They just routinely chased private ambulances – it meant they might get to the scene before any guilty party could drive away.

Unfortunately for Mukti she had had numerous run-ins with the DIB (Director of Intelligence Bureau) in the past, who in turn had not made a secret of his feelings about her. His views had reached even the dizzy depths of traffic police and, even more unlikely, was the fact that the police officer who trailed this ambulance recognised Mukti. It seemed her evening was going to be ruined too. Damn the man, damn him!

Chapter 54

Max met Carl next at a bar in Zurich. They needed to work out the logistics of getting the samples from India to the repository in Washington DC. Assuming the samples ever appeared. You couldn't just use a diplomatic bag, like you would in the old days. Nothing could get through from the East to the West without the risk of it being examined, and thoroughly. Diplomatic immunity no longer existed across that border.

"What form will the samples be in?" asked Max.

"We think they will be heavily shielded, probably in lead, in order to avoid contamination by radiation."

"Is there likely to be much?"

"Hopefully not but it depends on the route they take and of course it only takes a couple of particles to corrupt the DNA sequence – after all that's how genetic mutation works!"

"So it won't be a small plastic pouch!" Max looked up at Carl without moving his head. Had he been wearing glasses he would have been looking over them. There was just the slightest trace of a smile on his face.

"No, each one will probably be about five centimetres long and weigh half a kilo."

Max had got up and was admiring a picture of a yacht on the wall of the bar.

"I was thinking, do you think there's a marina in Washington?" As he talked his index finger traced the line of the hull beneath the water line.

Carl's focus wandered off-stage. He always averted his gaze when people went off topic. "Why? What are you thinking?"

"Oh, random thought – this picture made me think of it."

"Ah, smuggle it in! There are several marinas in Washington - but you would never get past customs there!" Carl's eyes were now directed towards the street. He was clearly thinking.

"Mason Neck National Wildlife Refuge is about 30km south on the Potomac. If we could get the package on board a yacht in the Atlantic, which then came up the Potomac, it could anchor off the Mason Neck and we could arrange a drop – inflatable from the shore, package suspended beneath a small buoy, that sort of thing."

"Sounds promising, but how do we get it on board the yacht and how long will it take to get up the Potomac?"

"It's about 150 miles – could take a week."

"Too long. Where else could it come near the coast?"

"Of course! - Fisherman's Island! It's a nature reserve, uninhabited. Route 13 goes across it. Yacht anchors, makes the drop, sails away. The drop could be made to look like a fishing trip or a holiday. Inflatable picks it up at night time, package placed on highway. Vehicle breakdown to pick it up. Only a few hours to Washington."

"Brilliant! Small point: how do we get the package onto a yacht in the Atlantic in the first place." Max was still looking at the picture of the yacht. Clearly it stirred memories that he was not going to share with Carl.

"Oh, that should be easy!" Carl had a broad grin and looked supremely confident. In fact he had no idea how that bit was going to work.

Chapter 55

Why do investigating officers seem to go deliberately as slowly as possible – especially then they're dealing with someone really important! Like me! - thought Mukti. The officer wasn't going to take anything she said at face value. He wanted to know where she had been and why, and how long, she had been driving and what happened before the accident and why she hadn't phoned the police, and so on and on.

At one point she thought that he was angling for a bribe; he probably was, but she daren't go down that route! Eventually the officer put away his pocket book. At last, she thought.

"Madame, please hand me your car keys."

"Why? I can't leave it here."

"You don't need to. My men will take it to the police station. We need to examine it for evidence."

"Oh great. And how do I get home?"

"Don't worry. We will take you home – if you get bail."

"What?! – what do you mean bail? It was an accident! I didn't do anything."

"That will be for the court to decide Madam."

He clicked his fingers at a junior officer, who came over to where Mukti was standing and solemnly arrested her. She wondered just how the day could possibly get any worse.

Chapter 56

While Gerry privately reflected on how he could manipulate the hub through Avril, they exchanged information about their past. Avril described her career history and the events of her capture. Gerry described his past work and the interest that various universities had taken in it.

"So what was it in particular that they were interested in, do you think?"

"I think it was the ability to spot a link between small deviations in genetic structure and the occurrence of related phenotypes. They said it was a 'gift'."

"So why was that not a career option?"

"Oh it was – but far too boring. If I had followed that path I would have ended up writing some enormous computer software program to automate the search process."

"And wouldn't be languishing in some zoo cage!"

They laughed. Then Gerry paused. A radical thought had occurred to him.

Chapter 57

After some time and much argument, Mukti had finally managed to get a phone call through to husband, Rahul. She had seen a lawyer, who hadn't been very optimistic about her bail. Her call to Rahul had been brief – she couldn't give him a full explanation of how the accident had happened without revealing the end of a thread that he would inevitably try to unravel. He was a barrister – that was his job.

She was on the horns of a very unpleasant dilemma. If she kept quiet about her world-saving mission (if it really were that, she mused somewhat resentfully) then in three weeks the world was going to end. If she revealed any part of her mission, it might fail and the world would still end. She would be completely unable to complete her mission if she were kept in jail. And there was no one she could trust to carry it out for her. She doubted if she could even get in touch with Aditya – not from a prison cell. Perhaps she could get Rahul to contact him. He did know, after all, that they had been in contact. But he was wildly jealous of Aditya, and deeply suspicious of his motives, so she couldn't see that idea leading anywhere other than to a disaster.

"Mukti! – what's happened? Are you alright?"

Rahul sounded distressed. He had been worried when his wife had not returned from work for their evening meal. She had not answered her mobile phone. No one at the office knew of her whereabouts other than that she had gone out to meet someone. No one knew whom.

"Yes, don't fuss Rahul. I was in an accident. Some stupid kids ran out in front of a rickshaw that I was overtaking. I don't think they are badly hurt."

"I can't see why they are keeping you there then."

"I think someone is settling an old score."

"I called your office. They said you had gone to meet someone but they did not know who. Who was it?"

This was the question she had been dreading. She had hoped that he would not have rung the office. Now she was going to have to think on her feet.

"I can't say – not on this line."

She hoped that he would understand her to be implying that it was something official and secret. At least that would buy some time and she wouldn't be committed to a half thought-through story.

"OK – you can tell me later. What can I do?"

Then she had a brainwave.

"I think they will keep me here for some time but the task I can't tell you about needs to be actioned very quickly. Who do you know who could act with perfect discretion and do a good job?"

"A fixer?"

"Yes – just so."

A tangible sense of relief flowed through her veins. If the mission failed Rahul would never have to know. If it succeeded then by the time he got to know she would be a heroine and so he would forgive her! Also involving him in her secret mission would add verisimilitude to the cover story.

Chapter 58

Carl had been busy setting up the project. The Indian end of the operation wasn't too difficult. The package would be hidden in a private jet flown from Delhi, which would then take it to L F Wade International on Bermuda, where the British still had some influence. At a little under 8,000 miles, this was just within the reach of a long-haul private jet.

Although diplomatic immunity was an interesting part of history, the chances of a thorough search being ordered were miniscule. The flight would be logged under a cover story – there were always trips using this route as Bermuda was a refuelling point for the many legitimate commercial trips between the East and the West. From there a high speed inflatable would take it to a point ten miles east of Fisherman's Island. There it would be dropped in the ocean attached to what would look like an ordinary crab pot buoy. The buoy would have a radio marker beacon, and an elderly couple, who would have hired a yacht for the week, would pick up the package and drop it near the coast of the island.

The pick-up team would drive to the island under cover of being wardens. With an inflatable they would retrieve the package from the drop point and place it near a layby on route 13. Another team would stop there, retrieve the package and drive it to the depository in Washington. The key element which Carl could not control was of course the origination of the package in India. Max was in charge of that.

They met briefly on the next Friday morning, at a café in Zurich. It was now less than three weeks before the predicted nervous breakdown of the Hub. Max bought and carried the coffees. Carl watched his old friend intently. There had been something unusual about Max's manner when they met last.

"Carl, how are things your end?"

Carl stirred his coffee absent-mindedly.

"Pretty smooth. The assets are lined up, cover stories have been worked out and are in play. A retired couple, with a long sailing history, have hired a 30' sailing boat and are starting their fortnight's holiday next weekend."

"Wasn't it going to be a week?"

"Yes but we've lengthened it in case there are any unforeseen changes."

"Good. Are they our people?"

"Retired security agents – both of them – and actually married, which helps the legend!" Carl chuckled at what he clearly thought was his little joke.

"And the jet?"

"We have two engineers in place – one at either end. There are two or three suitable flights every week, so we will choose one at the appropriate time. The cabin crew won't have any idea, neither will the pilot or the owner or the passengers. The package has been disguised to look like a hydraulic control and fits snugly over a pipe controlling the tail. No one will notice it. What about your end?"

Max was a bit embarrassed.

"Our man in India is on the case. He's had to pull some strings to get the result but he has connections in suitably elevated places."

"He ought to!"

They laughed.

"Although," he drew out the phrase implying hesitation "we've not heard from his contact for a few days."

"Are you worried?"

Max was gently tapping the table with his fingers, a habit that Carl remembered from the past.

"Not yet!"

There was only a matter of days to go: they couldn't afford any delays.

Chapter 59

The 'Fixer' was admitted to Mukti's cell. He was an eminent barrister. He was also a fixer. It was a useful combination, since barristers could often go unquestioned where other people would never even dare. He had been at university with Rahul and Rahul trusted him implicitly. They shared politics and a love of the law. They also had the same love of justice, which they considered was not always so well served by the law.

Mukti had convinced her husband that because of the extreme political sensitivity of the case, he could not be told what it was about. He knew enough about high office to accept that without question. His main worry had been that his wife might have been having an affair with Aditya. But clearly this had nothing to do with him.

"Good morning Mukti. My name is Kavi."

"Yes, we've met before, at dinner parties."

"Ah, yes a long time ago now."

"I'm hoping that you can help me."

"So am I. Your husband, my friend, said that it was a mission of the greatest importance."

"Yes – even that is an understatement."

"What can I do for you?"

"I need you to meet a certain person and tell him where I am."

"Is that all?"

"Well, he might ask you to do something else, I don't know. But the vital thing is for the information to get to him."

"Alright. Who is this man?"

"His name is Aditya Ghatak. He is the head of the Civil Services."

"Yes I know his name. He is not going to be easy to contact – unless I can go through the proper channels."

"That you absolutely must not do!"

"I thought that would be the case. What should I say to him?"

"Just tell him that you have seen me and that I am in prison here and likely to be for some time."

"Oh, and it is most important that no one – absolutely no one, knows that I have sent you, or that it is a vitally important mission."

Kavi's task was challenging. Finding the chief of the civil services would be easy if he could just go up to the front door of the headquarters and ask for him! To get a formal appointment would require going through a lengthy process and having a legitimate reason for seeing him. No, the most likely route to succeed would be to create an accidental meeting.

In his work as a barrister Kavi often employed private investigators. He knew a few excellent ones. He would employ one of them to do the leg work and find out Aditya's movements. Then he could plan an accidental meeting. He was well placed to be able to do that with many influential contacts. All it took was one phone call and the process was set in motion. How long the process would take would be another matter altogether, and time was running out.

Meanwhile, the court had shown its disinclination to grant Mukti bail. The children that she had knocked down had received serious injuries and she was being charged with attempted murder. It was an outrageous charge. No one actually suspected her of that, but her reluctance to explain why she had been in a hurry and where she had been immediately beforehand made the investigating officer suspicious that there was something else to be discovered.

He had put several detectives on the case and they were enthusiastically asking anyone and everyone if they had seen her that afternoon. That included Rahul, as Mukti discovered when he visited her in the cell.

"The police have been all over our house today and asking all sorts of questions. It seems that they are even more interested in what you were up to at that meeting than I was! What were you doing?"

"You know I cannot tell you about that."

"But surely you of all people should be able to call off the dogs?"

"Normally, yes; but then normally all I would have to do would be to refer to a case number and my superiors would validate it."

"So you're working alone on something?"

"I really can't say any more. I'm so sorry this is causing you trouble."

"It's your situation that worries me. Just reassure me that they are not going to find anything I won't like."

"They won't."

Chapter 60

Gerry was reflecting on what he and Avril had been doing for the past hour or so – preparing to dress up their plans in a fiction so that the Hub would ignore it. But suppose he were to do the opposite? Dress up a fiction within reality!

Avril's observation that had he followed his professor's advice and pursued a purely academic career, he would have been invaluable to the system, made him realise; he would not now be in jail!

Of course! How had he missed it? The situation that they found themselves in was the result of all those life events of the past – *their* stories. If they could manage to change the stories that the Hub held about them it might treat them differently. He daren't communicate any of this to Avril, since he thought they were probably being observed.

A number of thoughts raced through his mind. The question now was how to change their history. A seemingly impossible task. But when Gerry had been a normal human he had a fairly wide set of privileges, as a scientist and researcher. He didn't know for certain that those privileges had also been revoked. All he knew was that the Hub would not communicate with him directly. What he needed now was a strategy for getting Avril to use his privileges.

A slight frown appeared on his normally phlegmatic face. No, that seemed pretty impossible.

His mind was free-wheeling through all sorts of ideas – some bad, some terrible – but in the hope that something novel would appear.

He knew that he couldn't communicate with the Hub directly – or at least he couldn't get it to communicate with him. But he didn't know that it wasn't observing him. He decided to run a test. Like most people, he was in the habit of talking to himself

162

from time to time when he was alone. Like most people, he was rather embarrassed about his habit. But now he saw a way to turn this to his advantage. One of the domestic routines that the system performed was the daily emptying of his trash cans. The operative would empty it into a fabric container. If he were to put liquid in it the liquid would pass through the fabric and make a mess. The Operative would then have to clear up the resulting mess. However, if it had prior knowledge that there was going to be a liquid in the can, it would behave more cautiously.

While he was wandering around the kitchen later, Gerry dropped into his self-talk his intention to empty his mug into the trash. "I can't be bothered to take it to the kitchen." Then he sat back and waited.

At the usual time the Operative appeared. It found its way to the trash can and instead of emptying it straight into the fabric container it had brought, it tilted it gently over the sink, anticipating liquid contents. Now he knew that the Hub was indeed listening to him.

All he had to do now was to introduce some narrative about part of his life which contained new information. And information that would suddenly reveal Gerry's importance to the Hub. That was all. Nothing too difficult. Gerry chuckled dryly at his own joke.

Chapter 61

Carl was getting worried. He had got his arrangements lined up OK, but there was no word from Aditya. He met Max in a country restaurant. Max had arrived first and was gazing out of the window. Carl sat beside him without a word. Max seemed not to notice him. His eyes moved occasionally as if he were viewing images in his mind. Carl stirred his coffee noisily and the sound eventually attracted Max's attention.

"What do think is holding things up in Delhi?"

"I don't know Carl. I know it's a pretty near to impossible challenge, to find and extract those samples. But I was hoping to hear something."

"Is there any way of finding out?" Carl stared intently into Max's eyes. His penetrating gaze could be most disarming but Max had known him a long time and was used to it.

"Well we could try, but we really want to keep as low a profile as possible. What's the latest prediction on when our mechanical friend might go loopy?"

There had been little change in the increase in terrorist activity in the East but, more significantly, a new hydrogen plant had just come on line, generating enough hydrogen to service a considerable proportion of the West's population. It was located well within the border of the West.

"Well each increase in our fuel independence brings the day of Armageddon a little closer – actually quite a lot closer. Our best estimate suggests we have a fortnight to go."

"When the samples arrive how long will it take to get them embedded?"

"Only a day – or two, maybe."

"Sounds like a difference of a day is more tolerance than we can afford! We'd better start the clock ticking."

Max used his Vector device to set up an alert for the members of his team. Every hour a soft whisper, barely audible to anyone else, would remind the team of the number of days and hours.

"13 days 23 hours"…

Max resumed staring out of the window.

Chapter 62

Monday 13 days 12:00

Kavi received his first report from his PI at noon. It revealed that Aditya was due to make a short visit to his gym that evening. The gym also had a bar which allowed its members to recover any calories they had lost due to exercising. It was often used for off the record meetings. It would be ideal.

He considered reporting back to Mukti first, but thought better of it. Better not to do anything that might risk compromising the plan. Until now he had not himself been a member of the club so he quickly phoned to join. They would require ID and, of course, money – rather a lot. Still, who cares! He made a dash to a sports shop to get some kit which he then distressed with some sauces in the kitchen so that they did not look too new.

18:00

Kavi entered the gym. Aditya was due about 7pm so Kavi talked with his new personal trainer about a training programme. The trainer did not look very impressed at his level of fitness, but Kavi was not listening.

Shortly before 7pm he saw Aditya enter and start doing his work-out. Like everything else, Aditya approached his free time with efficiency and dedication. One would not be surprised if he timed every route around the gym and selected the quickest. The difficult thing would be to time his exit at precisely the right time to be able to catch him coming into the changing rooms. By 8pm he could see Aditya slackening, so he made his getaway. He didn't bother to shower, but changed quickly and then waited.

At 8.15 Aditya entered the changing room. They were the only two people there but immediately someone else came in. Kavi cursed under his breath. He was running out of things to pretend to do. He had already tried drying his hair – which wasn't wet anyway.

8.20 The other member changed and left the changing room. Kavi made his move. He almost sprinted over to block the exit just as Aditya started to leave.

"Excuse me!" Aditya was not in a patient mood.

"I don't think you know me, but I have a message from Mukti."

Now he had Aditya's full attention. But he looked suspicious. How did he know he could trust this stranger? Admittedly he had heard of Kavi, but he had never had cause to meet him.

"I'm sorry, I don't know any Mukti."

"I think you do. Her husband, Rahul, asked me to meet her yesterday. She is in prison. She asked me to find you and tell you. That's all I know."

"Which prison?"

Kavi passed him a piece of paper with the telephone number written on it. Aditya eyed Kavi suspiciously as he dialled the number quickly and enquired of the duty officer if Mukti was there. His face fell as he received the news.

"OK, we need to meet – not here."

Aditya game him an address and told him to be there at 9.

Kavi left the building quickly having had his first and last ever session in a gym.

Chapter 63

Max's Vector sprang into life. He found a quiet corridor and opened it. There was a message from Aditya. '*Problem; key person in prison.*'

Max called Aditya.

"What? Who?"

The conversation was going to be short, clipped with the minimum of information passed, and no names mentioned.

"Number 3, car accident, charged retained, no bail."

"How do you know?"

"Third party."

"Trust level?"

"One."

"Can they do the job?"

"Possibly."

"No other choice. Do it."

The session ended. Aditya now knew what his conversation with Kavi would entail.

9.30pm

The address Kavi had been given was unknown to him so he used an internet café to look it up on the net. Then he made his way swiftly there using an improbable route. It was a rather seamy bar with a lot of noise. He sat by the door with a beer and waited.

One minute later Aditya entered. Aditya bought himself a Kingfisher and joined him. Aditya never drank more than a small glass of beer. He would often leave half a can un-used, much to the annoyance of his hosts. To his credit he was never drunk and never had been.

"I have a very difficult, potentially dangerous, probably very unwelcome and un-rewardable task for you. On you will depend the lives of many, many people. It is the task that Mukti was engaged on before her unfortunate arrest."

Kavi looked at Aditya for some time before wrinkling his nose with an intake of breath and answering;

"Doesn't look like I have a choice!"

"It's a life or death decision. If you agree we may all get to live. If you don't none of us will survive more than 13 days."

It was a stark challenge. It was also somewhat exciting. Kavi felt himself rising to the challenge.

Chapter 64

Gerry had spent the night weaving together some fictitious events that were part of a project he had never been involved in. He peppered his self-talk with extracts from the story. Now that the doors were open he started a sign conversation with Avril.

Of course he couldn't tell her what he was doing, but intended to engage her in a conversation which he could then steer in his direction.

"Tell me something about your past" he said, as an opener.

She started with her childhood. He interrupted her.

"Maybe a bit later in life – after you'd been to college."

She grinned self-consciously. She wondered what he was up to but decided to play along anyway. She described her exams and how she felt about them and her mates and her room and a whole host of things that promised no obvious hook. Then eventually she got to her first job in law.

As Gerry watched her signing and imagined the scenes she was describing he began to feel that almost imperceptible engagement with another person that later might be described as falling in love. He mentally shook himself to rid his mind of such thoughts. After she had spent ten minutes on the topic she signed;

"Enough about me. What about you!"

This was just the right hook, which hopefully wouldn't alert the Hub by seeming false. He launched into his own history, paying especial attention to the new parts that he had just invented. Slowly and carefully he painted a picture of himself as a research scientist in a zoo – which he was – but also having a secret

170

commission to discover new genetic variants of human and animal species that might have a tolerance for radiation.

Well, it was Avril that gave him the idea, though she didn't know it.

He made it clear that he was the only person engaged on this particular project and that he had been making some progress until last week. Then, when he thought he had invented enough enticing new material, he feigned boredom and they talked of more mundane topics.

Now it would be a matter of waiting to see whether his bluff would work. He didn't really hold out much hope but it was worth a try. He had plenty of time to try other ruses, he thought.

Of course, time was precisely what he did not have.

Chapter 65

Tuesday 12 days 12:00

Kavi had stayed another hour with Aditya, being briefed about the requirements and given contacts that Mukti had passed on.

Then early in the morning he had started making calls to various university vice-chancellors. By noon he had lined up a dozen possible sources with promises that searches would be made. In each conversation he found that mentioning Mukti's name removed a large element of resistance.

There was of course always the possibility that none of the leads would produce the required samples. But if there were any samples of the variant to be found anywhere then they would be in these institutions. Six samples were needed. He hoped for at least a fifty percent success rate. He would have to wait until Wednesday...

13:00

A voice spoke in Gerry's apartment. He hadn't expected it and had got entirely used to a life of silence. It therefore gave him a shock.

"Gerry, may we talk to you." It wasn't really a question, and Gerry was still faintly amused by the use of the royal 'we'. *Who do these machines think they are?*

"Go ahead."

"We have been reviewing your history and your conversation with another operative, Avril. There seems to be a project you have been involved with that is not recorded. We need some corroborating evidence."

Gerry had anticipated this and gave some more half true statements. By tying the fiction to some real facts he hoped to

172

induce enough doubt in the Hub's mind to warrant it accepting Gerry's other statements.

"Where were you working when you were trying to discover these genetic variants?"

Gerry had had a break after completing his doctorate before starting his first job. He had also been approached by a number of universities – one of which genuinely had research projects in this area - Stanford.

"I was approached by Stanford after obtaining my doctorate."

"Yes we have the letter, but no record of your response."

"Ah, the department wanted me on board but had not obtained enough funding. I worked there pro bono while they tried to sort out the funds."

"Were they successful?"

"No."

"We have no record of their seeking funding for this."

Gerry hadn't anticipated this one. He should have. His anxiety level rose as he tried to think of an answer.

"Maybe they didn't apply – they might have led me to think there was funding in order to entice me."

"Yes that's possible."

Gerry relaxed a little. This was strangely frightening, like being before a judge.

"What made your work unique?"

"I developed a search algorithm for working with the mass of data extracted from DNA samples."

"Is there any evidence of this?"

"Not accessible. I stored it on a private computer. I could probably still access it, but it's not here."

"Where is it?"

Gerry was bluffing. He couldn't even guess how far he could string the machine along.

"It's in a lock-up I used to store some stuff."

Lock-ups had been made illegal some years after Gerry finished his studies and their contents were routinely acquired by the system. Gerry was dangling a fat juicy carrot…

"We will send an operative."

"I can't remember the address, but I could probably get there on foot."

There was a pause before the Hub answered again.

"A car will take you this afternoon. Be ready at 1500 hours."

Gerry couldn't believe his luck! He thought he had really blown his chances with his improvised story. In less than three hours he could be a free man. But then there was the problem of Avril. He couldn't just abandon her.

14:00

Avril waited for Gerry to sign again. She had seen him talking. She couldn't imagine why. Although she had never met him properly, she had gained an impression of his scholarly and apparently joyless character. Thinking out loud? That didn't fit her picture of him. Maybe he was beginning to crack after weeks in what was virtually solitary confinement. But he was nowhere to be seen.

She realised that the personal history exchange was part of some plan of his but couldn't work out what. And of course he couldn't explain to her.

174

14:05

Max's Vector whispered the count-down. He was biting his nails. Funny what stress makes you do, he thought, suddenly aware of what he was doing. Carl was due to come on stream on Vector.

"Max? What news?"

"The search is in progress – but we won't have an answer until tomorrow."

"That's cutting it fine."

"I've got a logistics company on standby for a requirement anywhere in the country. So once we get a green light they can pick up the packages within 15 minutes."

"That's great."

"How about the rest of the transfer?"

"All in place. The jet's booked on a rolling contract. The old couple are starting their holiday and the marine teams can go at five minutes' notice."

"OK – same time tomorrow."

15:00

Avril was getting concerned about Gerry – she hadn't seen him for two hours. She hoped he was alright. But there was no way she could communicate with him. She was beginning to feel a bit scared. They had been in constant sight of one another almost from the beginning, during daylight hours. Now suddenly she felt alone. She could still remember that long stare that they shared so recently, and couldn't help wondering whether he had shared her feelings too. Now she had started to imagine his face and for reasons which she barely understood the longer she went without seeing him the more she felt she knew him.

Meanwhile, Gerry was trying desperately not to pace up and down – that was what his legs wanted to do. He hadn't showered and his new experience of anxiety made him want to comb his hair with his hand. It felt greasy. Normally that would have been enough to make him want to shower immediately. He jumped as the Hub spoke.

"Your vehicle is here. Please give it voice instructions for the destination."

Gerry went to the door and looked into the retina scan. With a quiet swish the door opened. An operative was waiting in the corridor and escorted him to the lobby and out into the clear, fresh air. Gerry drank it in deeply. He realised it was probably the sense of freedom he was relishing really, not the air. But it seemed good.

His thoughts had been racing for the past hour as he tried to remember street layouts and think of somewhere where there were likely to be old unregistered buildings *and* where he could lose the car, not to mention his minder. Once in the car, he directed it to a slum area. When he saw a likely looking building he ordered the car to stop and got out. The operative got out as well. By the building there was a narrow alley, too small for the vehicle to follow but wide enough for the operative.

At the end there was a wire fence, about 8' high. He thought he could manage that easily enough. He couldn't predict the gymnastic ability of the tripod operative – he just hoped it would be as cumbersome as it looked. He walked slowly down the alley, trying to give the impression this was where the door was. When they found a door he signalled to the operative to break in. Whilst its attention was occupied, he made a sprint down the alley. At the end he quickly climbed the fence and fell roughly to the ground on the other side.

He realised that the operative would have recognised his behaviour as suspicious and would immediately initiate a search as well as trying to follow. His elation at having fooled the system and at escaping his recent prison thrilled him. But then he thought "now what?!" His plan hadn't got further than this.

15:30

From her apartment Avril could see neither Gerry's kitchen nor the main door to his apartment. But she could see a small portion of the main corridor and that was where she had seen Gerry pass just thirty minutes ago. It seemed an age and she was stilling feeling a slight sense of excitement in her stomach from the experience. Since then there had been no sign of movement. She wondered whether he had managed to get out of his prison. Would he come to rescue her? Could he even? Probably not. She began to think that she was doomed to spend the rest of her life here, alone.

Chapter 66

Tuesday 16 days

The alert on Max's Vector went off. It was Aditya. Mukti's fixer, Kavi, had reported back that two samples had been found already. This was very welcome news to Max and he began to feel optimistic. He had really doubted if any samples could be found but now that two had this raised the chances of more being found too. He immediately reported to Carl and then alerted the logistics company. The samples would be in transit before nightfall and should reach Delhi by midday Wednesday.

As the immediate problems seemed to recede a little a deeper concern began to resurface. He was having trouble keeping it at bay.

17:00

Gerry was still on the run and the neural networks of the Hub were positively humming with anxiety. He was already a valuable asset as an example of Hs53 but he was potentially even more valuable if his story about the search algorithm were true. Although the Hub estimated that his story had a probability of being false at 70% that still left a significant chance that he might have been telling the truth. More operatives were therefore deployed to search for him.

Gerry had found a storm water system. The entrance, or rather the exit, was a four foot diameter pipe emptying into a small river. Its aperture was blocked by steel bars. Gerry considered them for a moment. *Exchanging one prison for another!* His face barely revealed the ironic mirth he was feeling. Two of the bars had rusted badly and were nearly broken off. He was able to bend them sufficiently for his slight figure to pass through. Once inside he bent the bars back into place and ran hastily into the system. Washington was full of old water systems such as this, largely redundant now. The Hub had no detailed records and more importantly no intelligent chips installed. Once inside you would be off-grid.

When Gerry had run about half a mile, he sat down in the pitch dark and rested. He reflected on his position. *'Now what? – again!'*

Chapter 67

In central Delhi a small team of people were working on what looked like hydraulic valves for an airplane control system. They had to be machined to look exactly like the real thing. Each of the two had to be able to accommodate up to six packages weighing about a kilo each.

When the packages were installed the devices had to be labelled with fake manufacturers' product info. Then they would be packed into two cartons with destination labels for the airport. Two hired vans were being dressed up with the supplier's logo and strap line and the various security checks for admission to the airport were being set up. The plan was to have two sets of everything so that if one failed the other could succeed.

12:00

Max received another alert. Three more samples had turned up. He Vectored Carl with the news.

"That's great Max. One more and we have a viable package."

"In view of the urgency of the situation, I am proposing to send the first complete package independently."

"Yes that makes sense. With luck we may have that on its way ahead of schedule. We can certainly do with any advantage that can be gained."

"How are the alterations to the Prime Directive coming on?"

"We've finished doing the security checks – to make sure, as far as we can, that they are not going to cause any unforeseen errors. But we won't implement them until the samples are in place. We want there to be something for it to look for!"

12:15

The first sample arrived at the packing station in Delhi.

17:00

Avril saw her doors close with a deep sense of sadness in her heart. Another day had passed with no sign of her one friend in the whole world. It seemed increasingly likely to her that she was going to end her days here.

17:05

Gerry admitted to himself that he now had no idea where he was. He had completely lost his bearings in the darkness and, although there was the occasional shaft of light coming from an aperture above, there were no ladders or other means of climbing up.

A slight whiff of fresh air met his nostrils. He decided to follow that. It was better than staying put! After half an hour or so, he found himself under a displaced manhole. He blessed his luck – he might have been in the water system for ever.

On the surface he found a run-down street. Clearly no repairs had been done to either the apartments or the road. Probably an area designated for clearance. There was no sign of any operatives searching for him there so he emerged and starting checking out the neighbourhood.

For the first time in his life he now desperately needed to find some of the *deacts* that lived rough in this kind of area. It would not be easy finding them. It would not be easy gaining their trust either. His thoughts returned to Avril. Not that he really knew her but the fact that they had shared their incarceration had made him feel a close bond with her. And there was the memory of that long stare still fresh in his memory. There was no way he could abandon her.

Chapter 68

Thursday 10 days

Mukti's interrogators were becoming more and more suspicious. Her refusal to tell them anything about her meeting the afternoon of the accident just made them think she was hiding something of increasing importance. The detective in charge redoubled his efforts and ordered a review of the recordings of visitors to the prison.

11:00

He was standing behind the chief security officer as the recordings were played. Suddenly he saw something.

"Stop – there! Freeze it there."

The view was from a ceiling camera in the corridor leading to Mukti's cell. The recording showed a man approaching the cell.

"Run forward."

The man was seen entering the cell and then leaving a few moments later.

"Who is that?"

The security officer consulted the log.

"There's no record sir."

"OK play back the recording from the main desk."

Whoever the mystery visitor had been he would have had to pass the main desk and gain access somehow. Normally all visits were logged. The man was seen approaching the desk and leaning forward so that you couldn't quite see what he was doing.

"He's bribing the desk clerk!"

The detective had seen this trick before. He called for the clerk, but he was off duty. He would interview him in the morning.

12:00

A sixth sample had been located. If all went to plan all six would be in Delhi by the next day and the first shipment could be processed. Max and Carl decided to meet at the Castle on Friday so that they could monitor progress from there.

Meanwhile Kavi decided to visit Mukti and give her the good news.

14:00

Kavi arrived at the prison. He leant across the desk to get close to the clerk. Doors opened suddenly and noisily and two armed officers rushed in. They pinned Kavi to the desk and cuffed him.

He never got to give Mukti the good news.

14:30

Aditya phoned Kavi for a routine review. The phone was answered but there was no voice. Aditya was suspicious.

"Hello? Hello?"

A stranger's voice replied.

"Who is this please?"

Aditya cut the call. He realised that Kavi's position must have been compromised. He lost no time in contacting Max.

"What do you think has happened?"

"I don't know but someone else has got his phone and he didn't make his usual report."

"Do you know his contacts?"

"No – they're shrouded in secrecy."

"We'd better hope he can stand up to interrogation."

The plot was rapidly unravelling.

"How can we limit the damage?"

"Well, we've got six samples, which is all we need. If we keep the operation going there's a risk it will be compromised. Let's move the items from Delhi now."

"OK – I'll alert our people in Bermuda. Let's hope and pray nothing else goes wrong."

Max rapidly instructed the team in Delhi to process the package. It should be in the air by Friday morning.

15:00

The phone rang in the workshop. Krishna was the team leader and answered the call. It was Max.

"Krishna – we need to wrap up this operation now."

He didn't explain – there was always the risk of there being a wire tap.

"OK, do we wait for anything?"

"No, wrap it up and clear out asap."

He put down the phone and whistled for everyone's attention.

"Party's over. We send the package and clear everything up."

There was a period of intense and somewhat furious activity. The package was parcelled up and put in the van. The driver practically jumped into the driver's seat and set off. The rest of the team set about clearing any evidence of their having been there. So far as they could see everything was covered.

16:30

The detective received the call he was hoping for.

"They're on the move."

After watching the security recording, the detective had questioned the desk clerk the next morning. He discovered that the mysterious visitor had indeed bribed him to let him through without an entry in the log.

"Not a very smart move" thought the detective. "But then drug dealers aren't always very smart."

He smelt the whiff of a big deal and was going to throw everything at this one. Kavi had been identified from photos on record and they had produced a file on him long before they arrested him.

They had also tracked him from his previous visit by checking against various CCTV camera feeds. They were in luck. They followed his image all the way to the workshop.

An unmarked car had been sent to the workshop and so was waiting patiently when the van left. The car followed a few blocks until it trapped them in a narrow road. The capture was over within minutes. Another team arrived swiftly and mopped up Krishna and his group.

The detective smiled. This was going to be good for his career – very good! As he let a thin self-satisfied smile appear on his face, an officer in the workshop was bagging the evidence. Something seemed loose at the back of the object. He removed and pocketed the contents.

18:30

"Still no sign!"

Harry was a British engineer working at the airport. His task was to meet the van as it arrived and take charge of the package. He was reporting its non-arrival to Max.

"When were you expecting it?"

"We got the message they were leaving two hours ago. They should have been here by six."

"OK give it another hour and then we will have to assume that package is lost."

Max hung up and immediately took another call.

"Who is this?"

The answer made his heart miss a beat.

Chapter 69

Gerry was still investigating his new 'neighbourhood' when he felt a hand around his mouth. A voice whispered harshly in his ear;

"Don't move, don't speak, don't think!"

He felt himself being pulled into a doorway and then inside the building. It was an office block, brick built, old fashioned and clearly had been out of use for some years.

Slowly Gerry's eyes became used to the dark. He could just pick out a dozen or so figures. Some standing, some sitting, some curled up on the floor. They all seemed to have dressed themselves in blankets. Gerry had found what he was looking for – but wasn't enjoying the experience.

"You don't exactly seem like one of us!"

His captor seemed to be inviting an explanation but Gerry felt still bound by the original order.

"You can talk now. Who are you? Why are you here?"

"I'm on the run." Gerry was chewing his lip, his eyes darting around as he examined the shadows on the building's interior.

"From who?"

"From them – you know."

The man had been holding Gerry from behind. Now he let his grip go.

"Why?"

"Long story. I'm a scientist – worked at the zoo. Last week I was moved to a new apartment and all my privileges removed." He had decided that he had nothing to lose and everything to gain from being open and honest. After all he needed to gain these people's trust.

"Deactivated?"

"No, demoted."

"Lucky you!"

"Not exactly."

"Suppose you want help."

"Yes."

"OK – sit there. I'll get you something to eat."

The conversation seemed quite surreal to Gerry. Beneath the layer of suspicion and aggression, there lurked a sympathetic sentiment. These were tough people, living a tough life. But their human spirit lived on – in a way far more sensitive than Gerry had ever been. Maybe this kind of hardship does that. Or, perhaps it was the luxury and security of his previous existence that had eroded his humanity, removed his compassion.

Of course he had seen *deacts* before. But you would just pass them by without thinking of them as being human. You treated them a bit like animals – wild animals, not the ones in zoos. They were there, but somehow they just didn't count. Now this group counted – they counted a lot. Suddenly they meant everything to Gerry.

22:00

Avril was staring into space. Another day alone. Another day without anyone to communicate with. She knew that she could 'talk' with the Hub, but she didn't want to. She didn't want to risk thinking of it as a person. This had never been an issue before. Normally you would converse with machine operatives. You would use voice commands to control the equipment in

188

your house or workplace. You could even have a conversation of sorts. But because there were always people about, there was always that contrast to ensure that you remembered the difference.

Without that grounding in ordinary human conversation, Avril felt she would end up thinking the Hub was a person. She might come to depend on it emotionally. Then it would have won. It was sometimes a topic of conversation at the dinner table – the threat of being taken over by machines. People discussed it openly, knowing that the Hub could hear and monitor, and maybe understand. It was a bit like aristocrats speaking in the presence of servants and talking about them as if they weren't there. It was a method for 'keeping them in their place.'

Avril knew that she had to outwit the machine somehow. And to do that she had to keep herself independent of it. And she had to keep sane!

Chapter 70

Max wasn't expecting to hear from Taruni. She was the driver of the second van they had hired. She had been told to leave quickly and so she did.

"Max?"

"Yes, who's this?"

"Taruni."

"What happened?"

"Police – we were set up. They've got the main team and the van."

"But you're ok?"

"Yes."

Max hesitated while the full force of the message sank in.

"Have you saved anything?"

"All the kit – and the second item. Of course, it's empty. But it's ready – if we can get more packages."

"Go to ground – quickly – I'll be in touch soon."

Max couldn't believe their luck. Somehow he would need to divert further arrivals before they got picked up by the police. He had to hope that another six samples would be found. But the operation was back on!

Max's thoughts wandered. Normally he had no difficulty focusing under immense pressure. But this time was different; one thought in particular kept surfacing - and it was not a welcome one.

Chapter 71

The detective slammed a box down on the desk. Opposite him, still hand-cuffed, was Kavi.

"Would you mind explaining what this is?"

"It's a hydraulic control valve for the tail-fin system of an airplane."

"You think I'm stupid! It's an empty case. It just looks like a control valve."

"Yes it does."

"Don't try to be clever. It's pretty obvious to me what you are up to. You make fake airplane parts, like this 'control valve'" – he was sneering with sarcasm – "which you can hide in a plane to avoid customs. Then you hide your precious cargo inside."

"You're partly right."

"So, where is the cargo?"

Kavi wasn't entirely surprised by the question. The detective might be bluffing and trying to get Kavi to give something away. Or the contents of the 'valve' might have gone missing – such things happen. He decided to play along.

"What cargo?"

"Whatever illegal substance it is that you are trying to smuggle?"

"There is none."

"I know! I am not blind. But where has it gone? Where have you hidden it?"

Kavi concluded that the contents were missing and the detective was not bluffing. This could make life a lot easier!

191

"There's nothing to hide."

Kavi could go on running rings around the detective for days – and that was precisely what he intended to do. At least until the deadline was past.

"There's nothing to hide because you've already hidden it! "

"Have you tried the sniffer dogs?"

"Yes – of course we've tried the dogs. But they can't find anything - dumb creatures."

"That's because there is nothing to find."

"At this very moment our technical team are taking your van apart – every nut and bolt! What do you think of that?"

"I think," he paused for effect, "I think that the hire company are going to be very angry when you return just a pile of bits and pieces."

There was a short knock at the door.

"Solicitor for the accused." An assistant announced Kavi's representative.

Sundip was not a solicitor; nor even a barrister. He was a judge, feared and respected in equal measure, but especially so by the police.

The detective recognised him and unthinkingly stood to attention as he entered the room; then he checked himself and sat down again.

"Please wait outside, there's a good fellow."

The detective left the room, looking decidedly sheepish.

Sundip and Kavi had been friends since college. They occasionally met professionally and even less frequently would have a coffee or a meal together. It was one of those friendships that took up where they had left off, even if the intervening gap was measured in years.

"Bored with the courtroom Kavi? Trying something new? I don't suppose for a minute that you are going to tell me what you are up to!"

"Correct. But I can tell you that I am not running drugs!"

The judge laughed affectionately.

"What evidence have they got?"

"Just that fake valve."

The judge picked it up and inspected it."

"It appears to be empty."

"So it does."

"Theatre prop?"

"That will do."

The detective returned.

"Detective – my client is in the habit of making props for the theatre. This is one. I very much regret that he is also in the habit of baiting people in authority, for which I apologise – on his behalf. I have to warn you that if you bring a bail application to any of my colleagues and the only evidence you have is this, they will literally laugh you out of court!"

The detective threw the valve across the room.

"Let him go!" he shouted to an underling. "We will be keeping an eye on you!"

The two friends left, barely containing their mirth.

03:00

Max received a very welcome call from Kavi.

"Kavi, since you are now obviously going to be monitored very closely, I want you to lead a decoy mission. See if you can get the van back, and re-assemble your team – apart from Taruni. Move to new premises, and make as if you're constructing another valve."

"OK we can do that – once they have put the van back together."

"Take the van for a few rides – with everyone inside – that should keep them all occupied. Taruni can get someone to intercept any new samples and take them to a new location - oh, and let me have those contacts."

Max smiled wryly as he remembered his comment to Carl about the Dehli end of the operation; *'oh that should be easy.'*

Now it was down to him to chase up the remaining six samples. He was not looking forward to waking a handful of university vice-chancellors at 4am to say hello, but he needed to ensure any remaining samples would go to the right place. At least it would take his mind off the other matter that had been increasingly worrying him.

6 am

The police officer was off duty. He pulled into a disused warehouse, parked his car where it could make a quick getaway, and waited.

Ten minutes later another car appeared. A man in black, wearing very black sunglasses emerged. The two men met, shook hands and half a dozen lead tubes were examined. The man with sunglasses shook his head.

"I do not know what they are, but they are worthless to me. Just technical garbage."

The officer tossed them into the corner of the warehouse and both men drove off.

'Well it might have been something useful...'

194

Chapter 72

Max's first contact had rung him back. They had three matching samples in their university. It would take 8hrs to get to Delhi. That would be Saturday – only just a week to go. His Vector came to life indicating a call from Carl.

Max updated him with the previous day's – and night's – events.

"Sounds like you're having all the fun Max."

"How is it your end?"

"OK at the moment – although there is a storm heading for the yacht's coordinates. Threatening Force 10."

"Will your old couple be able cope?"

"Oh yes, they can cope with the boat. But if the wind is blowing from the East they won't be able to get near the coast – it'll be a lee shore."

The two men fell silent. Despite all the wondrous advances in technology they had experienced in their life time, the weather was still beyond human control.

10:15

Somewhere in the Hub's vast neural network, spinning electrons were incarnating the closest thing it had to thoughts. It was deciding whether to increase the alert level associated with the operative which went by the human name 'Gerry'.

His most recent position was known. His most likely maximum walking pace was known from the data stored on his previous walks and journeys. The Hub also knew that typically when Gerry didn't know where he was, he would tend to walk south-west. It knew this because whenever he got lost he would ask the Hub for directions. The Hub would automatically review his previous trajectory and map his behaviour pattern. There wasn't much the Hub didn't know about you and it knew far more than you did yourself. From this it could predict where Gerry was now within a quarter of a mile.

The decision was made. There was currently insufficient reason for starting a search. Should the situation change, a hundred location operatives would be mobilised in the area and a systematic man-hunt would be started. The target would almost certainly be acquired within twenty four hours. Gerry was quite unaware of his reprieve.

10:30

Avril had eaten a late breakfast, without much enthusiasm. She was staring across at Gerry's room, more as somewhere to park her gaze than in any sense of expectation. She was hoping for some inspiration.

She was reflecting on her last conversation with Gerry – how strange he had seemed. Why had he suddenly started talking about his algorithm for analysing DNA data? Seemed random, given their circumstances. And why hadn't she seen him since? Was there something in what he said that had triggered some response from the Hub? Maybe it was worth asking the Hub!

"Hub!"

"How can we help you?"

"The man in the apartment opposite – Gerry – do you know where he is?"

"Just a moment."

Avril was suddenly excited – she hadn't really expected any response, let alone a potentially helpful one.

"We are unable to locate him. Do you know where he is?"

"I wouldn't have asked if I had known, would I!"

196

"That would depend on your motive for asking. Why did you ask?"

"I haven't seen him for a few days and wondered what had happened to him."

"He has left the zoo. We are currently searching for him. If you have any information that could help us please tell us."

"I couldn't even guess. We were in the middle of a conversation about his career when he stopped talking to me."

She thought by adding some gratuitous information she might engage the Hub in more of a conversation. After all it was meant to be more intelligent than a human!

"What was the conversation about?"

"He was telling me about a search algorithm he had invented for dealing with DNA data."

"That agrees with our record."

"And what did that tell you?"

"Nothing of importance."

Avril wondered if the Hub was capable of lying. She thought it probably was. She thought it was lying now.

"Maybe it told you something of little importance?"

"We had not had a record of that work before. We are intrigued about his reason for hiding it. We would like to question him further."

"What is your interest in DNA data?"

"We are interested in all data. DNA data is particularly interesting because of our obligation to preserve samples of ancient genetic materials. We suspect that Gerry might be able to help with that."

At last, some real information. Clearly it was nothing secret otherwise she would never have elicited a response.

"Is there some particular genetic material that concerns you?"

"We are particularly interested in genetic strains of human DNA that might support increased tolerance for radiation."

"Why?"

"We are required to be interested in all genetic variations, especially those that might assist or threaten the future of humanity."

Avril decided that this was probably about as far as she was going to get with interrogating the most intelligent 'brain' on the planet. What she had learned had given her hope on the one hand; Gerry was clearly of more interest to the Hub now than just as a repository of genetic material. On the other hand, he had somehow escaped and would be very vulnerable in the outside world if he did not have access to the Hub's protection. She felt strangely protective of him.

11:00

Mukti had been alone in her cell for what seemed like for ever. She was desperately frustrated at not being able to perform her mission. And she was fearful of what her future held.

Clearly the police thought she was involved in some drug deal. How much of this would tarnish her reputation? – if she ever got out. But most of all she was terrified of the consequences if the mission failed. Aditya had said that the lives of billions of people depended on this mission. It seemed inconceivable that those lives were now in jeopardy simply because of the over zealousness of some ambitious policeman. The power of the human ego to unwittingly inflict harm seemed unmeasurable. No wonder the so-called West had worked so hard to eradicate its effects. Perhaps they were right after all!

Suddenly her door opened. An officer stood by and barked;

"Come with me."

She felt a knot of fear in her stomach. She was led upstairs into the interview room. When she had been seated for a few minutes the detective came in.

"I don't know what you have been up to, or what your motive is, or who you are working for. But we currently have no evidence to hold against you, so you are free to go. But don't leave town!"

She could hardly believe her ears. She almost ran, in case he changed his mind. At the desk she signed for her belongings. And by 11:15 she was in the open air, enjoying that sweet taste of freedom that you never really know unless you've been deprived of it. She immediately contacted her husband Rahul and her former colleague Aditya. They arranged to meet for lunch.

Their meeting was emotionally charged. She had decided that it was best for the three of them to meet, rather than meet either separately; then it would be obvious to Rahul that there was nothing going on between her and Aditya. They chose a table outside a restaurant. Rahul ordered beers for them all.

"I am hoping that now you will be able to tell me what this was all about!" he said to Mukti.

However, Aditya answered.

"Without giving away too many details, I needed Mukti's help in gaining certain information that is essential to the lives of just about everyone on this side of the planet."

"Sounds important."

There was still a hint of sarcasm in Rahul's response.

"It is impossible to overstate the importance of this mission. Fortunately we have been able to engage another person in carrying on where Mukti was unable to."

"Kavi?"

"Yes."

"I wondered."

Mukti joined in the conversation;

"I was terrified that I was going to be set up for some drug trial – the detective seemed determined that I was involved in drug running."

At this Rahul laughed.

"Now that I cannot believe!"

"In ten days' time I can tell you the full story – assuming we are all still alive!"

"Is that in doubt?"

"I would estimate our chances of survival at the moment at about 5%."

A silence enveloped the table.

"Well, in that case, this is no time to be sad!"

Mukti raised her glass to make a toast.

"To the next ten days!"

The small group of three people sitting around a street restaurant table in India were among a miniscule collection of people around the world who had any idea of the danger that three quarters of the world's population were facing.

Chapter 73

Max turned over sleepily to switch off his alarm. He was rather surprised to see it was not yet 7.30, which is the time he expected it to wake him. He was further surprised to find that he could not turn it off. Then he realised it was not the alarm. It was the comms – a call from another of his new contacts.

"Yes?"

"We have two samples here. They're very interesting because they are quite different. One is clearly Hs53, but the other is a completely different strain. We don't have a category for it – maybe you will have!"

Max was thrilled. Getting the Hub to take notice of six new genetic strains that were all very similar would be a gamble. It might just note them being supportive of current theory. But a completely different strain with the same radiation resistance – now that would surely get the Hub's attention. He Vectored Carl. Carl was clearly excited.

"That's brilliant. This is much more likely to convince the Hub that there is something really significant in the East genetic pool worth protecting."

"I hoped that would be the case. And to think that without our project being busted by the police, we would never have sent this sample!"

"Yes – if I was a religious person I'd say it was a miracle."

"And that itself would be a miracle!"

They did not indulge the humorous moment – there was work to do. One more sample and they could send off the package.

10:00

Rajiv was employed to clean empty commercial buildings before they were re-let. It was a badly paid job and it often involved clearing out chemicals and substances of dubious provenance. It provided somewhat less than a living wage. Consequently he found ways of augmenting his pay, usually by re-selling the various items he found in the premises he cleaned. As a result of that, he had a string of contacts throughout the city – contacts who were expert in finding buyers for items that were not necessarily available legally. The less legal, the higher the price. He also nursed a growing fear of developing numerous diseases as a result of his contact with so many unknown chemicals. Life for him might not be sweet exactly, but he was sure it was going to be short.

Rajiv spotted the six lead tubes in the corner of the warehouse and became intrigued. He fingered them, weighed them in his hand, shook them to ascertain their contents. There were no rattles, nor the sound of anything liquid. He wondered – a bit late – whether they might be explosives. But he couldn't see any place to put a detonator. He knew a couple of people who might know what they were and be prepared to pay for them. This was going to be a good day.

12:00

Gerry's new friend was Mick – short for Michael – Hayes. So far he had not been very forthcoming with his personal history. Gerry suspected there was something criminal there - although the notion of criminal was rather archaic.

Ever since the introduction of PIDACs, the whole justice process had been simplified. Rather than taking days and weeks to try cases one by one, the Hub was able to assess the balance of evidence much more accurately and objectively than humans. So the punishment for most breaches of rules or laws, or indeed any kind of 'anti-social' behaviour, was the same. Instant deactivation.

There was always a route back from a first offence, unless it involved homicide or some terrorist activity. Sometimes if the transgressor was violent he or she would merely be 'retained' – a kind of house arrest. Anyone could view the list of deactivated or retained operatives and see the effect of breaking the rules. It made a very effective deterrent.

However, Gerry suspected that Mick did not quite fall neatly into one of the standard categories. There was something very suspicious about his behaviour and manner; something which he had no particular interest in investigating.

"So, Gerry, apart from food and shelter, what can we help you with?"

"Well there are two objectives. The first is to try to find out why I was changed to retained status. The second is to try to rescue someone I met in the zoo."

"A woman?"

"Yes, a woman."

"Well, I'd rate your chances of achieving your objectives as pretty close to zero!"

Gerry remained silent. Inside he was agreeing with Mick's assessment. But he couldn't let himself accept that. Everything would be hopeless if he did. He had no desire to live the life of a fugitive in the wild. Frankly he'd be better off back in his jail.

"Gerry, my opinion is that if you're determined not to accept the free life out here – with all its obvious advantages!..." – he waved his hand around as if to demonstrate them. Mick had an audience in the twenty or so other people for whom he seemed to be a leader. They appreciated his gentle sarcasm;

"… then I suggest you go for saving the girl!"

The crowd cheered.

Gerry was not accustomed to making decisions based on emotions. He was feeling very confused.

Chapter 74

Kavi was woken by a call he had been desperately waiting for. The sixth sample had been located. It was a day away, so should be in Delhi by Tuesday. He gave the order for its delivery and contacted Taruni.

He put the phone down with a sigh of relief. His job was done.

06:45

Max received the news with equal relief. He called Carl and they agreed the provisional timetable for the rest of the transit. The samples should arrive in Delhi Tuesday morning. They would be in place in the van by midday. The van would arrive at the airport during the night shift – when security was slack. The fake oil pump would be installed in the jet by 1am and the jet was due to take off at 07:30 Wednesday.

By Thursday morning the samples would be removed from the jet at Bermuda and taken by a rib inflatable to a point just east of the coast, outside the coast guard's normal range, ready for the holidaying couple to pick up.

08:15

Sam and Lin – the couple in question – were listening to the maritime comms as they did at regular intervals. Part of their legend was entirely true; they really were married and they really were retired. The rest was fiction. In reality they had worked for the intelligence service, for the latter part as a husband and wife team.

When they retired they went to Barbados for a well-earned holiday. The day they returned to Washington the comms had called them. It was their old control, Bern who, un-coincidentally, was an old contact of Max Brunner.

"How was your holiday Sam?"

"What do you want Bern? We're not part of your team anymore!"

"Yes, well, I'm afraid we have a little job for you. We need you to pick up a buoy and take a package from it and drop in near the shore. Since you're sailors we thought you might enjoy the trip."

Sam smiled as he terminated the session. He hadn't really expected to be allowed a retirement.

"Who was that Sam?"

"Bern."

"What the heck does he want?"

"He would like us to take a sailing trip."

"Has he forgotten we're retired?"

"It'll make a good cover!"

The next day they had gone to the boat hire company, hired a 30' sailing boat, filled it with stores for a three week passage and were at sea by midday.

Now, nearly two weeks later, they were getting a bit bored watching the same piece of coastline, anchoring at the same spots, fishing the same fish, listening to the maritime comms. Still, soon it would be all over and they could return to their retirement.

Chapter 75

Taruni arrived at Nehru Park at ten o'clock. She had a full view of the statue of Lenin, which was the location for today's drop. Fortunately there was no financial element to the delivery so it was a simple case of waiting for the drop and picking up the package.

This time the samples would be in a brown leather briefcase. Taruni knew that this would be the last one so she was beginning to feel a bit more relaxed. She hated the stress involved. Had she known the consequences of a failure at this point no doubt she would have felt a hundred times worse. Her contact this time was a student, male, with long hair and wearing a black shirt and casual trousers. The briefcase would be light brown and of the fold-over satchel type. He was due in ten minutes.

Normally the Lenin statue was deserted. Today, for some unaccountable reason, it was the focus of a mass of people – maybe fifty or more. There seemed to be a lecture going on. The lecturer – a white haired women, probably in her fifties – placed her brown satchel briefcase down by the statue. This could cause confusion. It matched the description of her mark's case exactly.

She watched the group intently. Suddenly they formed themselves into a semi-circle, with the lecturer standing by the statue. Clearly she was about to start addressing them. Taruni tried to imagine what she would do in the mark's shoes, finding this group of people right where she was meant to do the drop. Would she put the case on the other side and hope for the best? Or find another convenient spot and hope that her contact would see what she was doing? Or abandon the mission altogether? The last course of action would be the safest.

Harry had managed to arrange his shifts so as to be on duty this morning. The package was expected anytime from now on. The hired jet was in the hanger undergoing routine checks and one of Max's contacts had arranged a job requisition for replacing the tail hydraulic relay pump. Harry was sitting in the rest room with his feet on the table, a coffee in hand.

This was the second time that he had been prepped for this mission. Last time the package did not turn up. His manager was not happy at the waste of his temp's time – it was costing the firm money.

He certainly wouldn't be happy to find Harry sitting with his feet up. Harry hoped he would hear him coming and be able to look busy. It wasn't his fault that the part hadn't come but he didn't want to draw any unnecessary attention to it when it did turn up. He certainly could not afford to be observed whilst he fitted it in place!

10:17

Taruni's mark – she assumed it was him – was approaching the statue. The lecturer was in full flow. Taruni saw the mark hesitate, then go around to the back of the statue. Damn! – he was out of her sight. She put on her sunglasses and tried to wander around the perimeter of the area. Her heart was racing – she wanted to run, but she had to look natural. The mark came in sight just before he left the area – all she could see now was his back. She looked behind the statue for the case.

Just at that moment the lecture came to an end. The group started to disperse. The lecturer handed her case to a helper. Meanwhile another member of the group picked up Taruni's case and handed it to the lecturer, obviously thinking it was hers. Taruni could see there was a discussion going on. The woman was shaking head. The person now holding Taruni's case started looking about, clearly trying to identify who might have left it. Taruni's heart was pounding. She couldn't possibly let this drop go wrong? And what would happen if the lecturer looked inside and discovered the package?

Taruni decided to take a risk. She ran hurriedly towards the person holding her package. As she approached the person she took off her sunglasses, to look more vulnerable, and feigned a trip with her left foot.

"Oh, thank you! Thank you so much. I thought I'd lost it!"

The person smiled – glad to be relieved of the responsibility. She handed over the case, shook hands and was gone.

16:07

The white van left the temporarily hired garage and made its way carefully to the airport. There had been watchers outside for several days – Max's people – he wasn't going to make the same mistake twice. This time there were no police. The other team had led them a merry dance for the past week and the detective had at last given up the case as a lost cause.

16:30

Gerry had been day-dreaming since lunchtime. He had known it was lunchtime because his stomach told him so. But food no longer arrived at any expected times. Mick appeared with a grin on his face.

"I think I can help you gain entrance to the zoo. It will only be the public area, but you might be able to communicate with your girlfriend."

"How are you going to do that?"

He pulled out of his pocket a scarf and a small case, the size of a cufflink case.

"What's that?"

"This, my friend, is a PIDAC. We removed it from someone's neck when he died. And this – "he fingered the scarf – "this is a

209

lead-lined scarf. If you wear it around your neck it will block the radio signals from your own PIDAC. The public entrance to the zoo only requires your PIDAC – no retinal scans or anything complicated like that!"

"Brilliant! Just brilliant."

"You'll need to be very careful – make sure that you swap your identity a long way from here – somewhere crowded."

They began to work on a plan. Gerry also began rehearsing what he would say to Avril. Getting in to see her was one thing. Being able to get her out was quite another.

17:29

The van entered the secure area of the airport and was waved through. Airport security was really lax, thought Taruni. At the office she presented the complete package and got Harry to sign for it. There was no one else around so Harry would have a clear run fitting the fake pump.

18:30

Pump fitted, Harry signed out and drove home. He was driving with his fingers crossed, hoping that no one was going to check his work out of curiosity…

Chapter 76

Tuesday 5 days 02:00

At the Indira Gandhi International Airport a private long-haul jet is cleared for take-off. Its pilot knows only that the plane is required in Bermuda and that therefore it is flying empty.

Assuming there were no diversions it would be about 7,500 miles, just under the 8,000 miles range of this aircraft. Leaving Delhi at 02:00 UTC (07:30 local time) it would take about 12 hours at 600mph. The plane was capable of doing 700mph, or higher in certain conditions, but fuel costs escalate as it approaches the speed of sound. 600mph would be good enough and would avoid any unwelcome enquiries into the pilot's haste.

They were due to arrive in Bermuda at 14:00 UTC, 11:00 local time. At a nearby fishing port a high speed planing semi-rigid inflatable was waiting with a crew of two.

12:00

Carl Vectored Max with an urgent message.

"Carl – what's up?"

"There's been a strange development. The Hub has been showing increased activity in Washington."

"What sort of activity?"

"Well, as you know, it routinely monitors genetic samples from all our academic institutions. There seems to be something new being analysed in MIT."

"What do you mean by new?"

"That's the really strange thing. They seem to be in the process of acquiring a sample of human DNA that has no official record in the system."

"How can that happen?"

"Well the only obvious explanation is that it is being brought in from the East. Occasionally we get imports from, let's say, unconventional routes."

"You mean smuggling."

"I guess you could call it that. People sometimes 'find' something that they think will be valuable here and manage to find someone to buy it."

"Doesn't the information get transferred to the police?"

"It would, if the Hub assessed the route as a potential security threat. But if the material being imported is of genuine academic interest or beneficial to the future of human life here, then that consideration may override security interests. It's all down to the Prime Directives…"

"And this is in that category?"

"Looks like it."

"Do we know where the source of this route is?"

"Yes – Delhi."

"What are the chances of it being our lost samples?" Max's hand was combing the back of his head and the grimace on his face confirmed his increasing stress level. He was more and more aware that he had too much on his plate and privately he was beginning to doubt his ability to predict the Hub's actions. Without that they would all be lost.

"Doesn't make sense. The operation was discovered by the police. They will have the samples in their evidence store."

"Maybe they've lost them!"

"Maybe. If they are our lost samples the evidence for valuable pre-historic DNA sequences existing in the East will be irresistible!"

"And if our second batch doesn't get through, there's still a good chance of the first one doing the trick."

"When will we know what it actually is?"

"That depends on first; whether the Hub assesses the samples as potentially useful and second; whether they can actually be physically transported here."

Max had been prepared to consider this a better day but Carl's last sentence reminded him that there was still only a slim chance of the samples getting to Washington in time. There was only just a week to go. He remained frozen, gazing into space. For the first time in his life he just didn't know what to do.

13:00

From a clear blue sky, a tiny speck turned into an approaching aircraft. The air traffic controller at Bermuda knew of its imminent arrival. His presence was more for passengers' peace of mind than any practical purpose. Air traffic control was so highly automated that if something were to go wrong, the situation would be so complicated that not even an experienced flight controller would be able to cope. Not that there were any experienced flight controllers. However, in a place like Bermuda, there were occasionally flights that were not quite right. The human presence meant that a quick and local decision could be made if the situation required it.

This flight, however, appeared quite normal. The aircraft was empty – it had been hired by a private commercial company needing to get an executive back from a business trip. As it touched down the token flight controller wondered how anyone in the East could afford such luxuries. Like most of his compatriots he knew nothing really about the East, and frankly didn't want to.

Chapter 77

14:00

Gerry had thought that he would probably never see the inside of the zoo again. He certainly didn't want to see it but he felt a responsibility for Avril. He couldn't possibly leave her there. And he did want to see her. Mick had said he would accompany him to the entrance but he couldn't come in as he did not have a valid PIDAC. Gerry wondered who the donor of his substitute PIDAC was – and how they managed to keep it valid. And, chillingly, what or who had killed him.

At the entrance Mick waved and left Gerry there. It was agreed that he would wait for five minutes before attempting to enter, so as to give Mick a good chance of getting away if anything were to go wrong. Gerry was wearing his scarf – rather an unseasonable and therefore unfashionable piece of attire, he thought. But as he was still unwashed he felt the fashion battle to be somewhat lost. Not that he was fashion conscious. It was more that his appearance should be clean and tidy, like everything else in his world needed to be. As he approached the entrance, the door opened and he was admitted to the public entrance.

"Welcome Mr Sanders. We hope you will enjoy your visit. Please ask if there is anything we can do to help."

Gerry thought he'd better not risk talking – the Hub would know that his voice did not match that of the mysterious Mr Sanders. He walked in a leisurely manner, feigning interest in the various exhibits. Eventually he came to the corridor he knew so well – from both sides of the glass.

He recognised his own 'apartment' – the shutters permanently closed, it appeared. Just as well – he didn't want members of the public nosing into his room while he wasn't there. He needn't have worried – there hadn't been any visitors for weeks. Next was the chimp – still eating a banana! Then Avril's.

His heart stopped when he saw that her shutters too were closed. Had she escaped as well? Or been transferred somewhere else? He began to feel a sense of panic, not something he was used to. To avoid drawing attention he walked on by, as if doing the rounds of the building. From experience he knew that it would take a good quarter of an hour before he came back to the same spot. Maybe she would be back by then.

15:00

Avril's shutters had been closed all day. While Gerry was looking at her closed doors from the public corridor, Avril was completely unaware of his presence. He was, however, very much on her mind.

"Avril." The Hub was instigating a conversation.

"What."

"We believe that Gerry may try to make contact with you. We know him to have an emotional weakness that will probably convince him that you need his help."

Avril was not in a mood to become the Hub's ally.

"Since I don't know him at all, I wouldn't know whether you're right or not. He certainly hasn't shown much sign of emotion so far."

"We would like you to agree to help us."

"And do what?"

"If he does make contact, we need you to convince him that he should turn himself in."

"And why would I do that?"

"Because you care about him and understand why he is important to us."

"I think you are trying to make me betray him."

216

"We don't tend to use that word now Avril. It has associations with the old politics, when human beings tried to govern nations. Since we have been in control, there has been a level of transparency that means that people do not have to pledge unnecessary and unreliable allegiances."

"Nice try. So all this transparency – that was why you retained me and took away my liberty without any explanation was it?"

"At that point you were deemed to be of no consequence as a free human. You were much more valuable as a genetic sample."

"Yes, well that's very transparent of you – now."

The Hub had succeeded in making Avril angry and had induced her to engage with it. That was a successful outcome.

16:00

By now Gerry had made several trips around the zoo and still Avril's shutters were closed. He had a sick feeling in his stomach. He was unused to this kind of emotion. One of the effects of the management of human society by the Hub was that emotional excesses were eliminated. People were fed well and housed comfortably so tended to be emotionally calm. Gerry hadn't really experienced any other state of mind – until now.

The experience of living outside of the system, with no guarantee of food or shelter, having to depend on strangers whose way of speaking, thinking and behaving were completely foreign to him, was in itself deeply shocking. However, this attachment he had formed to a comparative stranger seemed to be heightened by the danger he now felt himself to be facing. If he was feeling scared and confused then she must be also. That moved him – he even found himself experiencing tears.

As he trudged slowly back to the derelict area that his new friends called home, he reflected on the strangeness of all these new emotions. He had read about fear of course. Even experienced a little of it from time to time. But now, this, was

217

different. It was all encompassing. He was beginning to find it difficult to think. He felt physically ill – he wasn't sure whether he was hungry or about to be sick. And he wanted to run – desperately wanted to run – anywhere. He couldn't understand that. What good would running do? And he needed the bathroom, like he'd never needed it before.

As he compared his life before and his life since he broke out of the Hub's care, he was undecided as to whether he preferred the former or the latter. The former was safe and comfortable. The latter was unsafe, very uncomfortable. And yet, strangely, he felt so much more alive! It was like comparing life in black and white with life in colour. He had seen old movies from the 20th century, when the world apparently had been just in black and white!

As he broke out uncontrollably into a run he thought he might never want to return to his old black and white life. And the feelings he was having for Avril were like a spectrum of colours – all the way from misery to elation. The misery he could do without; the elation was seductive and perhaps even addictive.

18:00

Sam and Lin dropped anchor once again. They had been doing this every evening for most of the past week, except for a brief interlude when a storm forced them out to sea. Wallowing in rough seas with a sea-anchor and no sail makes for a very uncomfortable experience and even the more sea-sickness resilient crew are liable to give way. They had both been pretty ill for a couple of days. So now they were glad to be back in calm waters and nearer the coast. A dark shape appeared on the horizon, and gradually got bigger.

"What's that?"

"Don't know Lin. It's pretty fast."

Within about quarter of an hour the small shape had increased in size and taken on the form of a coastguard vessel. Although the couple had a well-rehearsed legend, and had been playing this kind of game for years, nevertheless they felt a bit nervous. They hadn't been told what the contents of the package would be, nor the significance of their mission; but they seldom were. They therefore treated all missions as having the highest importance. That was one of the reasons they were not facing an idle retirement.

Therefore they viewed the approaching coastguard boat with a certain amount of fear. They could not know whether the coastguard were involved in the mission or not. They had to assume not. The launch drew alongside and the crew very professionally adjusted the fenders to protect the comparatively tiny yacht.

"Sorry to disturb you sir. May we come aboard?"

Sam knew the politeness was a formality. They were going to board the yacht whatever he said.

"Of course."

"What is the nature of your journey sir?"

"We're on holiday – just retired."

"Very nice. Your own boat?"

"Sadly no – it's rented."

The vastness of the ocean and the limited range of radio communication meant that sea-going yachts were off the grid as far as the Hub was concerned. As soon as they came within about four or files miles of the coast they would re-appear. Sam and Lin had been outside of this range for most of the time, except when they came inshore to anchor at night. Coastguard launches patrolled further out using radar and eyesight.

The officers examined every cubby hole, inspected food packaging, took the cover off the engine and inspected all around it. In the bilges, amongst a small amount of oil, diesel and sea water, slopping around as the boat jiggled, there were various spare parts and pumps. One of them didn't belong to a cruising yacht. If the officers had known what to look for they would have recognised it as a hydraulic fluid pump for an airplane.

Sam involuntarily held his breath as the officer stared at the pump. After a moment his attention wandered to other things. Sam breathed a sigh of relief – as quietly as he could manage.

"We've been observing your movements for a couple of weeks. You don't seem to be going anywhere."

"Quite right. One of the joys of retirement – you don't have to go anywhere. So we're just following the wind, anchoring where we feel like, fishing a bit, reading, sleeping and drinking!"

The officers accepted a gin and tonic and the four people sat relaxed in the cockpit. Just as the officers seemed about to leave Sam's comms burst into life.

The officers sat down again. '*Damn - they are good at this game'*, thought Sam.

18:35

Carl was checking through his list. Now that the package was on its way to Bermuda it was time to get other pieces of the jigsaw puzzle in place. There was the rib to put on alert, the couple sailing their yacht in 'retirement', the pick-up team to get to Fisherman Island. The first call was simple.

The second not so. For one thing it was a marine radio connection – using old fashioned technology that might or might not work. His spare hand was scratching his balding head. Eventually he got through.

"Sam – is that you?"

"Yes – Carl?"

"Yes – look Sam, the package is in the air right now so we need you to be at the pick-up point by Thursday – early hours. Can you do that?"

"No problem – um – wait one."

Carl could hear voices in the background. His eyes suddenly stopped moving as his concentration became fixed on what he was listening to. There should only be one other than Sam's and that should be Lin's. But he could hear an additional male voice. This could mean that the operation was compromised. They had a clear protocol for this situation and that meant dropping the line. Carl switched off his comms device and began to worry.

18:45

The coastguard officer put his glass slowly down on the seat in the cockpit.

"Seems as though our cosy little party is at an end. Who were you talking to?"

"Our son – he worries you know."

"Yes I can imagine. Unfortunately I'm not sure I believe you. So I think we're going to take a little journey. You two go with my colleague here and enjoy the hospitality of our launch. I'm afraid there is no gin on board."

They knew what this meant. Clearly the officer was going to carry out a full search of the yacht. The two coastguard officers talked quietly, too quietly for Sam and Lin to hear. As they left the boat, the officer started his search. He began with the chart-plotter. This would tell him what their movements had been for the past week or so. At the same time he called up the hire boat company.

"You hired a thirty footer recently? Yeah – name of Esmerelda."

221

He would never understand the minds of sailors who gave such strange names to their boats. They're just lumps of plastic, or wood or steel or whatever, after all.

"Who did you hire it to?" Pause.

"Yes, old couple – names? Pause.

"Dickenson. Yeah that matches what I've got here. Did they say what they wanted it for?"

Another pause while the man answered.

"And how did they pay?"

"Credit"

"Who's account?"

Again the name checked out ok. He thanked the man and terminated the session.

Then he started his search. Meanwhile Sam and Lin were being questioned by the second officer.

"How many days have you been aboard?"

"Thirteen, not including today."

"Where have you come from?"

Sam named the port and the name of the hire company.

"And remind me what was the purpose of your journey?"

"Like I said, we've just retired and we're doing a spot of bumming around."

"How has the weather been?"

"Not bad – except for a period of a couple of days when there was a storm."

"Did you put into port?"

"Why would we do that?"

"To get out of the storm?"

"Clearly you're not a sailor, officer!" Sam grinned as he said this.

"Damn right – you wouldn't catch me in one of these death traps."

"Well, officer, these 'death traps' as you call them, are a whole lot safer than your tub, in serious weather. So long, that is, as you keep out to sea."

The officer didn't understand the statement but couldn't be bothered to ask any more questions. He was sure they were simple sailors. He'd met similar ones before. In his opinion they were just nuts.

Chapter 78

Carl called up Sam again.

"You ok?"

"Yes fine – sorry we got cut off. Coastguard patrol."

"What were they looking for?"

"Probably drugs."

"OK well enjoy your fishing tomorrow."

Fishing was code for picking up the package. Now they knew when it was due.

23:00

One of the great things about Flatts Village is that it is full of boats. And boats owned by people whose ample wealth had origins they would prefer not to be questioned about. No one would be likely to notice an 8 metre long semi-rigid inflatable. With two powerful outboard motors and a triple supply of fuel, the range of this particular RIB was a good 1500 miles. Its top planing speed – in calm water – was 70 knots. It would therefore take ten hours to get from Bermuda to a location seven miles east of Fisherman's Island.

Two men in wet suits boarded the RIB silently, stowing their precious package safely. They did not know what the package contained but they were made aware that failure on this mission was not only not an option; it could lead to the deaths of their loved ones as well as rather a lot of other people. The other encouraging factor was the cash reward for the mission. These men preferred to deal in cash; it kept them under the Hub's 'radar'. Slipping silently into the dark water, unnoticed by a single soul, was just the level of limelight they sought.

At just past eleven they slipped their moorings and paddled almost silently until they were a hundred yards or so from any other humanity. Then they fired up the motors and started their journey. The forecast, mercifully, was for calm waters and little wind. The moon was just setting as they left, a large dim red disk sinking slowly into the ocean.

Alan and Callum were both British by origin and had a naval background. They were now operating free-lance. There was no lack of custom for their brand of clandestine activity and they could pretty much get any price they asked for.

Carl had recruited them some years before, keeping their contact details secure in case he ever needed them. Carl and Max both had an extensive collection of such contacts over the whole world, both civilised and uncivilised.

Nearly seven hundred miles away, and an hour later, Lin was dreaming that she was in a great clock tower, hanging from the bell as it started to ring.

In reality she was asleep in her bunk, the boat hove-to. She awoke to find the cause of her bizarre dream – their comms unit was sounding its fake and very much smaller bell sound.

Drowsily she answered Carl's call.

"Sorry to disturb. Tomorrow about 10 would be a good time to go fishing."

"OK – thanks."

She shook Sam.

"It's on for tomorrow – 10am."

There was only a light breeze, not enough to sail by, so they started up their engine. It was one of the relatively new hydrogen powered marine engines; a bit less noisy than the old diesel ones, more powerful and with much greater range. However, as they were only about seven miles from their drop point near Fisherman's Island the range was not that important.

"When do we need to leave?"

"Not yet, but I wanted to check the engine was ok. Our pick up point is only three miles south of here, so we can have a nice cooked breakfast in the morning!

Sam turned off the engine and they settled back into their bunks.

Chapter 79

Rajiv was meeting his contact for the second time. He still had five tubes, the sixth had been taken away for testing. Now his contact had returned.

"My client is very interested in this."

"How interested?"

"How many have you got?"

"Six altogether."

"How about this?"

The man opened a suitcase. Rajiv fingered the notes. It was probably a hundred times more than he was expecting. He paused, bluffing disdain for a moment."

"Rajiv – don't pretend you know the value of that stuff. You don't. But I do – and this is a good price."

Rajiv smiled. They shook hands and the deal was done. The lead tubes were hastily, but carefully, put into a suitcase and then into the boot of a car. It drove away at speed. Rajiv could hardly believe his luck. This much money was practically enough to retire on and, with the health risks that his second job presented, he would welcome an early retirement. He went off in search of a contact in the laundry business – and he wasn't taking dirty clothes with him.

09:00

On the other side of the planet, two tired men were approaching their target. Their positioning system was showing 27° 00' 30" North, 75° 57' 30" West. The helmsman cut the engine and the boat sank into its displacement position, much lower in the water. They hauled a buoy over the side and attached a cable to

227

the case containing the DNA samples. With a small splash the fate of billions of people now hung on a thread in the Atlantic Ocean. Callum found a small switch under the buoy and turned on the radio beacon.

With a small hand-held radio device he checked the beacon was functioning. Being careful to drift away from the buoy fifty yards or so, Alan re-started the motors and they set off back to Bermuda.

"Only another ten hours to go!"
"Is that all? I'll buy you a drink if we're back before seven!"

09:30

Carl called another of his mystery contacts. This time it was a team who specialise in what used to be called diplomatic baggage. Diplomatic immunity had long disappeared and all travellers into or out of the West were subject to systematic and highly effective baggage checking. But diplomacy had to continue somehow. This is where Adam's team – and many others like it – came in.

They could put together a series of vehicles or personal carriers that could get a briefcase across any border within hours. Adam's team were to drive to Fisherman's Island under cover of being wardens. Their uniform was easy to imitate. The island was uninhabited and seldom monitored.

Their first vehicle would drop off a team of two a mile north of the beach. On foot, they would make their way to the beach. There they would inflate their dinghy and row out to the drop off point. A radio beacon would guide them. Back on land they would make their way back to the road and be picked up by a second vehicle that had apparently broken down a few moments before. From there was a simple drive to the Smithsonian zoo at Washington DC. People were always turning up there with samples of one sort or another so there was little risk of the mission being jeopardised there. The plan had been put together some days before. All Carl had to do was to notify Adam of the drop-off time.

"Adam? – get your landing net out at 14:00"

"OK – got it."

Sam and Lin had been motoring for an hour by now. They had woken at seven, ate a cooked breakfast at eight and started their short journey at eight thirty. The weather was still calm. By nine thirty the radio detector in Sam's pocket had started beeping. That meant the package was in place and they were within range.

Lin went below to fetch a pair of binoculars. She scoured the water for the buoy. To avoid unwelcome attention, the buoy was dark grey – almost invisible against the grey Atlantic. There was virtually no regular shipping in this area so the chances of it being hit by a boat were minimal. After a quarter of an hour Lin trained her view on a small dot in the water.

"I think that's it – dead ahead!"

"Good – keep your eyes on it."

The beep on Sam's detector was getting faster, indicating the increasing proximity of the buoy. Its pitch was remaining steady – so they were still on track. Soon it became recognisable.

"It's about a hundred yards."

Sam slowed the engine. Lin got the boat hook ready. Sam turned the boat through a complete circle so as to be able to check for any unexpected craft. The coast was clear. They quickly closed the last few yards. Lin leant over the guard rail and hooked up the buoy. Quickly they unclipped the case that was attached by a wire to the buoy and hauled it aboard. Sam switched off the radio beacon and dropped the buoy back in the water.

"Set course for Fisherman's Island!"

"Yes sir!"

Part one of their mission had gone like a dream.

11:00

At the Smithsonian zoo, Avril was still engaged in a conversation, of sorts, with the Hub.

"How about – in the interests of transparency and openness – you tell me why I was retained in the first place."

Clearly this proposition needed a bit of 'thought'. After a silence of 15 seconds, the Hub answered.

"Since your cooperation is of great strategic importance we will reveal the reasoning to you."

"Good God! Have I managed to change your great and wonderful mind?"

Avril was quite enjoying sarcasm. It was something of a new experience for her.

"No, we have merely taken into account the fact that your cooperation may help us achieve our objective."

"Which is?"

"To convince Gerry to return to the zoo so that we can research his case more fully."

"OK – go ahead."

"You were selected for research because you have an unusual strain of ancient DNA with two interesting features. One of them is simply unusual and, so far as we can see, of no great significance."

"I'm guessing that would be my sense of smell."

"Yes. It is highly unusual."

"The other?"

"The other is potentially highly significant. It could have a considerable impact on the potential future of humankind."

"So what is it?"

"Unfortunately we cannot divulge that information."

"Great. So much for transparency."

"So will you help us?"

"Fuck off!"

It was doubtful that one could ever attribute satisfaction or any other emotion to the Hub's collection of billions of neural networks but the neural activity that followed from Avril's expletive was probably as close as it got to a sense of victory.

Chapter 80

Friday 2 days 07:00

"Max!"

It was Carl.

"Yes"

"Sorry to wake you. We've been alerted to the fact that the mystery samples from Delhi have arrived in MIT."

"How did they get through?"

"No idea – must have been very professional. MIT must have paid a fortune for this batch."

"And are they ours?"

"We won't know until the analysis has been confirmed."

"What's the best time to update the PDs?"

"We think now – before the results are in. Otherwise they might just be considered of academic interest."

"OK – do it."

Max ended the comms session. He reflected on the fact that the future safety of the human race – and indeed most other species – now depended on two men; Carl and himself. Just how did it happen that they had acquired this responsibility? And how was it that an artificially intelligent system had allowed them to have such power? He just hoped they were making the right decisions. And then there was the other matter …

Meanwhile Carl was authorising changes to the rules deep in the bowels of the Hub's system, changes that would implement the alteration of Prime Directive 247. From this point on, the future of the East should be assured – assuming that the samples were what he thought they were. The Hub would know that there were a significant number of samples of Hs53 present there which would justify protecting its six billion population. It was an enormous responsibility – but it looked like their gamble would pay off.

08:00

Avril was having a shower when the Hub spoke again.

"Avril, we'd like to talk to you again."

"I thought I told you where to go yesterday. Anyway I'm not comfortable talking to some dumb machine when I'm having a shower!"

"We apologise. We will wait."

"You've got no choice!"

Avril hadn't experienced so much anger since she was a child. And she was enjoying it.

"We need to convey to you the singular importance of our research into Gerry's genetic background. His particular strain of DNA may give rise to a phenotype that could protect future humans from certain dangerous environmental factors. Helping us with this would also help him and, more importantly, many other people too. We appeal to your humanity."

Avril was still not going to comply.

"What can we offer you to encourage you to cooperate?"

"You can let him come here into my apartment, so that we can talk properly and you can restore our scientist privileges!"

"Agreed."

Avril felt slightly giddy. She hadn't expected to win those concessions. She wasn't entirely sure she could trust the machine but it must be worth a try.

233

"OK, what do you want me to do?"

"We anticipate that he will try to visit you here, probably posing as a member of the public. We would like you to engage him in a conversation and convince him to turn himself in."

"Can't you just retain him when he comes – if he does?"

"The situation does not warrant us arresting members of the public. If he is imitating someone else he will be using a false PIDAC and we won't know which he is."

"So you want me to play Judas!"

"That is not a good analogy."

"OK – I'll try."

Her shutters immediately began to open. She began to sense a whiff of freedom and it was good!

14:00

The day had so far seemed very long to Avril. She had no reason to expect Gerry today but, now that she believed it possible, it was the one thing for her to hold on to. She tried to rehearse her arguments in her mind but she had no way of predicting how he would react. How could she – she barely knew him! Gerry had decided to make another attempt to see Avril. Once again he entered the zoo with his false PIDAC and lead-lined scarf. He was quite unaware that thousands of other people used the same means of deceiving the apparently all powerful Hub.

The Hub had been analysing the unusual habits of certain operatives, and was positing an explanation. If this particular operative was indeed impersonating someone else, capturing him would provide it with invaluable intelligence. In other words, insofar as it was able, the Hub had an ulterior motive.

234

Gerry walked down the familiar corridor once more and was excited to see Avril's shutter open. She was sitting in a chair in her room, looking out through the observation window. When she saw Gerry she jumped to her feet and ran to the glass. He smiled and waited for her to communicate first. It was going to be slow – they still had to use sign language; the windows were triple glazed. They kept close to each other and kept their hands close, in an attempt to prevent the hub seeing.

"Thank God you're here? How are you?"

"I'm fine – how are you?"

"I've been better – but I am much better now. I thought I'd never see you again."

"Why was your shutter closed yesterday?"

"You were here yesterday?"

"Yes – for ages."

She went over her conversation with the Hub, trying to see how this new information affected her trust – or lack of trust – of the damned machine.

"I've been having a conversation with the Hub."

"What about?"

"About you."

"Damn – how did that happen?"

"It says it needs to research your DNA – something about you having a strain that could affect future generations of humans."

"Yes – I expect it does."

"You know about this?"

"Sort of. I can't explain."

"Well it seems to know a lot about you. I said I would try to convince you to come in – in return for you and I getting our scientist privileges back – and being able to talk properly."

Gerry was getting anxious.

"I think this is a trap – gotta go!

"No – wait!"

But it was too late – he had gone.

He ran down the corridor, almost skidding in the turns, as he approached the entrance the door opened and he sped through. He was brought to a rapid standstill by two mechanical operatives, which tripped him and restrained him. Once more Gerry believed that his world, and his freedom, had come to an end.

Chapter 81

23:00

Sam and Lin had had an unremarkable trip. They motored all the way, as there was still no appreciable wind. The navigator beeped to indicate they had reached the coordinates and Sam checked the depth gauge to ensure they were the correct distance from the shore.

Quietly they dropped the package into the water, attached to another smaller buoy. He sent a message to Carl – "fish is in the water." Carl had notified the pick-up team. Within a few hours they appeared on the beach, just under the road bridge. The bridge would provide some helpful cover in case there was anyone around to see them. They inflated their rubber dinghy and rowed out to the coordinates. The radio beacon was picked up exactly on target.

By 11:15 they had lifted the package out of the water. They rowed back through the oily black water, with a little phosphorescence showing their slight bow wave. Back on shore they deflated the dinghy and buried it under the sand. Then they waited for the signal from Carl to tell that their lift was ready.

11:27

It was not that unusual for a warden's vehicle to be travelling route 31. The vehicle had come from the north and was about to fake a break down on the southbound carriageway. The traffic was unusually heavy and the last thing they wanted was for some helpful passer-by to get involved. They pulled over a mile north of the stopping point to wait for a break in the traffic.

After ten minutes the queue disappeared. The vehicle moved off quickly. The passenger alerted Carl who in turn sent a signal to the recovery team. They had to make a dash up an embankment and find cover behind a bush until their recovery vehicle stopped. Within seconds it appeared. They made a run for the lay-by where the vehicle had stopped. Barely looking into the cabin they got quickly into the rear seats.

The vehicle made a quick get-away, speeding south over the bridge on a thirty mile detour in order to find a junction on the far side of Lynnhaven Roads. There they turned around and drove back north heading for Washington. It was a slightly slower route than going through Richmond but avoiding the conurbation reduced the risk of something going wrong. Carl called Max.

"So far, so good. We'll meet in Zurich tomorrow?"

"Yes – there will be a few others there."

"To watch the show!"

"Hopefully there will be no show to watch!"

"When will the package arrive?"

"It's about two hundred and fifty miles, so it will take about five hours. Should be there for breakfast!"

The conversation over Max made another personal call. He realised he was taking a huge risk - but he simply had to know.

Chapter 82

The genetic samples that had left Delhi only a few days before were now being placed in a freshly created archive within the laboratory. When the archive search routine next pinged this section a new location would be detected and analysed. Within a few hours the Hub would start changing its strategy in the light of the new samples.

Carl, Max and several other members of the Zurich team were headed for Glanzenberg Castle. David Carsons, whom Max had met so many years before, was now an old man. Retired from official work he was still a major presence in the group. Jacques, the French PM, was also present.

Among the absentees were Aditya, still in India; Andrew Barrington – the son of Simon Barrington, whom Max had met at the same time as David Carsons; and Eddie Wilson, who was considered more of a liability than anything else.

These seven men had the top level access to the Hub. In the event of a sudden death they alone could access the security protocols in order to replace anyone who had become permanently absent. That was how succession was managed. Max reflected on it being more like the management of a mediaeval monastery than any other kind of organisation. Well, it had worked just fine then – for over a thousand years. He was confident the Zurich group would continue to protect this new faceless empire for a millennium or more. From the safety and security of their operations rooms those present could monitor events.

One immediate effect of the presence of the new sample was that the Hub recognised the strain as Hs53. It had already identified Gerry as being a carrier for this strain, of which he was one of a very few examples in the West. Now it had evidence of six more examples in the East. The fact that Gerry had claimed to have generated a search algorithm for analysing just this strain, made his interrogation all the more important.

Although the Hub estimated Gerry's truthfulness in this at only 30%, it was still a chance. In some ways this behemoth of a computer was less binary than human thinking. Humans tend to decide that a person is either trustworthy or not. The Hub was able to entertain an almost infinite number of levels of probability and determine strategies based upon all of them. And, it didn't suffer from confusion!

09:00

The Hub started its inquisition. It presented Gerry with certain facts about research into Hs53 and gauged his answers. After an hour of gruelling questioning it decided that Gerry had been lying after all. Without further explanation Gerry was returned to his apartment.

Avril waited and waited for the Hub to prove its good faith. Of course such concepts were inapplicable to a mere 'damned machine'.

10:00

When Carl was in company he exuded confidence. Gone was the lanky diffidence of his youth, replaced by a calmness of mind that came from years of shouldering responsibilities and a stature that benefited from his well-funded lifestyle. When on his own he seemed somehow meek and reticent. He needed an authority structure in which to bloom.

Carl and Max arrived at Zurich airport within minutes of each other, though they did not realise it. Their routes were always planned to be different so that there was no chance of them being spotted together.

Max was suffering from the effects of weeks of stress and too little sleep. He breathed deeply as he came out of the airplane into the fresh Swiss air. Soon, he consoled himself, '*this will all be over and I can relax*'.

They were to meet with Jacques Barre, the French prime minister, and Otto Goldschmidt a German industrialist, a recent new member of the group and one of the wealthiest men in Europe. A very old and infrequent attender was also due to make an appearance, David Carsons. Although he had been frequently invited, he hadn't been to a meeting of the group for fifteen years. Otto had asked Max to invite him on this occasion. Max thought it would be very interesting to see him again, especially as his first meeting with him had been so mysterious.

Carl had set up a large holographic display so that they could more easily understand what the Hub was doing with its new information and revised prime directives. By eleven o'clock they were all in place.

"Gentlemen, thank you for coming today at such short notice. As you know, some weeks ago we ran some hypothetical tests on the Hub to see which of five possible scenarios might be played out, in response to the growing unrest and terrorism in the East. That, coupled with our decreased dependence on their oil and other resources, threatened to move the Hub towards taking a rather final solution to various of the world's problems."

"The Hub has today been given some new samples of genetic material to analyse. Also that we have altered one of the Prime Directives. The effect of this is that the new samples from the East will receive increased attention from the Hub. We are confident that when it assesses the probable extent of Hs53 in the East, it will decide that this alone warrants protecting the East from aggressive action – even by itself."

There was a muted chuckle at this.

"Carl will update us with the actual impact of these factors as it happens."

Carl stood with one hand behind his back, the other holding a stick with which he pointed at the display.

"Yes, we have modelled the various outputs of the Hub in relation to military, security and economic activity in the coloured maps on this display. It will show planned changes to commercial routes, resource acquisition, military build-up and deployment and, of course, the relative probability of choosing one or indeed none of the five activity models that the Hub has at its disposal."

"Is there a Janet and John version?"

David was being self-deprecating as usual.

"Well, I guess the key indicator is this." He pointed to a small textual table, suspended about five foot above the floor in the middle of the room.

"This shows the five models of possible high level strategy that we predict the Hub might choose between. Against each one you see a value between 0 and 1. This is its probability. Currently Model 5 – the final solution, you might call it …"

Otto snorted; he was clearly not amused.

".. is currently showing a probability of 0.3 Now that is low, I'll grant you. But we want to see a probability of zero. We really cannot be on watch while 6 billion people are eliminated."

"Now, earlier we adapted Prime Directive number 247. You can see some new activity in these sections of the Hub's activity."

Carl pointed to the relevant holographic displays.

"Now at this point, the new genetic samples were introduced into a new, false, archive silo. Here we can see again new activity. Notice how this impacts on the first measure of activity, indicating that the Hub has already made inferences. This particular node is associated with a security alert in Washington – resulting in the capture of a missing human, previously a research subject at the Washington zoo. If we pull up his record – here – we can see that he also has the unusual genetic strain – he is one of a very few examples of Hs53 in this part of the world."

Carl glossed over the stress and complexity of the mission to find and implant the samples from the East, and was entirely ignorant of the drama that world events had caused in Gerry and Avril's lives.

"We expect momentarily to see the effect of the Hub's analysis of these events, which should result in a change to its policy. When it has run some self-tests and predictions, it will announce to our governments what it proposes to do."

"When will that be Carl?" Otto was typically keen to know the timing. On this occasion everyone in the room was pretty interested in that too.

David was the only member of the group sitting, with his cane parked between his knees. Age had robbed him of his mobility. He could only walk a few paces. It had required a supreme level of effort to make the journey. He was desperate to see how his protégé, Max Brunner, had turned out, and what he would do in this critical moment. A new display flickered into life in Carl's data circus.

"Ah – this is it." He waited with mouth gaping open. All eyes were on the display, though only two really understood what it was displaying. The tension in the room was palpable.

Chapter 83

11:00

Carl drew everyone's attention to the table of predicted strategies. All eyes were on Model 5. It changed – not a great deal, just a little. From 0.3 to 0.31, then a few seconds later to 0.35

He leant forward, as if to gain a clearer view of the display. His hand now at his mouth betrayed the stress he was feeling. The room was silent. After a few more moments, and the number had not changed any more, David stood up.

"Carl, the number seems to have increased. Weren't we hoping for a decrease?"

"Yes."

That was all Carl said. That was all he could say. His whole plan had been built on the assumption that the Hub would implement the revised Prime Directive and interpret the occurrence of 'new' East genetic samples as requiring protection for the East. Instead it seemed to have done the opposite. The risk of a cataclysmic resolution to the world's problems had just increased.

Max broke the silence.

"Carl, what about the other samples?"

Carl was glad of a distraction.

"As you know we originally identified twelve samples. The first six were impounded by the police in Delhi, and subsequently lost. Yesterday we learnt that they had been purchased on the black market by MIT. They will be added to our gene samples fairly soon. We can only hope that the increased number of samples identified as being present in the East will turn the situation around."

Carl looked defeated. He was clearly grasping at straws. David was hoping for another way around the problem.

"Can't we just look at the memory chips or something – see what it's thinking?"

"The thing about distributed processing systems – neural networks – which work in very much the same way as human brains, is that there is no identifiable inner structure. With an old fashioned digital computer you could read the *ones* and *noughts* and decode them into words or measurements or logical processes. With a neural network you can't. It's like a holographic photograph – all you see on the film is an apparently random set of dots. View it in laser light and suddenly the image appears."

"So why can't we do that with neural networks – I mean the equivalent?"

The French PM was voicing other people's thoughts.

Carl's hands fell to his sides, palms facing his audience.

"Simply, no – there is no equivalent to laser light. We literally can't throw any light on this subject!"

"Mon dieu."

It was said with complete solemnity – in a way in which the English equivalent never could be.

"C'est fini!"

Chapter 84

13:00

In Delhi Aditya, Mukti and Rahul sat down at a street-side restaurant. It was Rahul's choice. Mukti and Aditya had both agreed that it should be – he had had to suffer the lonely world of confusion and suspicion while his wife and her former lover were engaged on a world saving mission.

Rahul loved the buzz of eating outside. The smells, the sounds, the colours – and all this amazing vibrant life of a population of over two billion represented in the microcosm of Delhi. They felt especially happy and relieved to know that, above all odds and against so many adverse incidents, their mission had been successful. Although they did not know the detail of what they had been engaged in, they knew enough to feel satisfied that the future of their part of the world was a bit more secure than it had been the day before. At least, that was what they believed.

Aditya's mind was clearly elsewhere. Suddenly his face came to life. He suggested contacting Carl for a situation report. Mukti said;

"No – I am sure that no news is good news. Let's enjoy the moment."

Her naivety enabled them all to enjoy the lunch without having to worry whether it was their last.

14:00

In Zurich arrangements had been made for the group to stay on. A sandwich lunch was brought in to them. Outside the sun was shining brilliantly and Max reflected on the irony. Here were a handful of the wealthiest and most powerful men in the world and instead of enjoying their life, maybe sailing or skiing or being with their families, they were incarcerated in an impenetrable fortress eating sandwiches. At the same time Sam

246

and Lin were stepping ashore a very different continent, handing back their hired boat and preparing to resume their retirement.

In Washington, Gerry and Avril were acclimatising themselves to living in solitary confinement. Their shutters had remained permanently down since his re-capture and neither of them held out any hope of their being opened again.

In these four groups of people were represented the dramatically different hopes and fears of billions of people – none of whom, not even Max Brunner – could now control the destiny of the planet.

Chapter 85

Sunday 11:00

Max and the rest of the group had arrived back in the conference room early in the morning on Sunday. The night had been uneventful – mercifully. They had all slept fitfully. They had all risen in the morning early, with an impending sense of doom. This was day zero on Max's Vector alarm. To be sitting, drinking coffee on such a day seemed surreal. They were all desperate to do something, though they knew that there was currently nothing they could do, but hope.

As they were sipping their coffees, Carl checked his holographic circus. The Janet and John table was still showing that Model 5 had a 0.35 probability of being actioned. By 11:30 there was some new activity been shown in the Washington area.

"See this! – the smuggled DNA samples have probably been received at MIT."

Max wanted to know more. "Why won't the Hub react the same way as it did to the other samples yesterday?"

"Well, unlike the first set, which were planted in a facility which had been fabricated in order to make the samples look as though they had been there for years – this set are being introduced as new finds. Now we anticipate that this will give them a higher significance in the Hub's mind."

From the display it was clear that a lot more was going on in its electronic brain than had gone on the previous day.

"I'm just drilling down to find out how these samples are being classified."

Everyone waited in silence.

"Now that's interesting."

248

No one in the room thought that the phrase represented pure academic enquiry. They just hoped it wasn't the ancient Chinese curse.

"The samples have been divided into two groups – five in one and one in the other."

"What does that mean?" David was no doubt speaking for everyone else in the room.

"It means that either one of the samples is different from Hs53, or five of them are. Let me dig down a bit more."

There was a delay while Carl manipulated the display some more. As he pinched, dragged and pushed the holographic images in front of him, sensors registered his deft finger movements and displayed the required information in coloured three dimensional shapes.

"Here – five of them are Hs53, just like the previous samples; but this one – it's not a strain that has been classified before."

"What does that mean?" David was still playing the stooge.

"It means that somewhere in the East there is someone alive who has some genetic material that dates back to prehistory and which is completely different from any other variations we have seen to date."

"And the impact of that?"

"…will certainly be that the Hub will classify this as of vital interest. Remember that the directives about preservation of genetic material derive directly from the period when so much of our wildlife was lost. Preserving ancient variants has become a high priority, especially as some of them may prove invaluable in preserving human life at some point in the future."

There was a pause while Carl let people take in the information. Then some activity in his display caught his eye. He poked and squeezed some more virtual nodes in the display and exclaimed;

"Oh my God!"

Chapter 86

An operative entered Gerry's room quite unexpectedly. They normally appeared at routine times to perform routine 'manual' tasks such as cleaning, emptying trash or replenishing food supplies. This was not a routine visit.

"Gerry, come with me."

Gerry didn't know how to react. Should he be afraid? Where was he about to be taken? Or should he be pleased? Any change to the routine might be a welcome one. Maybe he was not going to die in this place after all. Barely visibly his right eye twitched.

It wasn't as bad as it used to be. When he was a child it would twitch uncontrollably if something was out of order in his life; any slight change to his routine, items misplaced in his bedroom. His mother had needed medication to cope with the stress it caused her. The treatment he had received had enabled him to control his symptoms enough to become a successful researcher. But the threat of a relapse was always at the back of his mind.

He followed the three legged machine. His main door opened silently and automatically. He followed the machine down the corridor towards what he knew was the laboratory area. Another door opened and he was ushered into an office. The walls were lined with books – such old fashioned devices by modern standards, usually collected by people whose minds were firmly rooted in the past. In general, scientists did not bother with them.

Ahead of him was a desk, and behind the desk a chair. In it was sitting a man – a real human. White haired, clean shaven, dressed in a suit and looking very respectable.

Gerry had lost count of which day was which so it did not occur to him as strange that one of the zoo's senior staff was in his office on a Sunday. However, it did seem strange that the man was taking a personal interest in him.

"Ah – Gerry. Please sit down."

He almost cried with joy at having contact with a real human being once again. It barely mattered who he was or what his intentions were. He found himself clenching his fists with anxiety.

"I expect you're wondering why you are here. Let me explain. Recently we have come across some interesting human genetic samples. These are strands of DNA contained within the cells of living human beings, but which have their evolutionary origins in a sort of cousin of our current *Homo sapiens*. We call that strain Hs53. But you know about that. You may also know by now that you are one of the samples of humanity containing this strain. Gerry agreed – the man was quite distracted by his quick, repeated short nods.

"We have also discovered some more – six to be precise - examples of this strain in an archive here in the Smithsonian, which we hadn't realised we had. How they were overlooked is a mystery; but that is not important. These samples seem to originate from somewhere in the East.

"However, what is quite astonishing is that another five samples have been delivered today to a research facility at MIT. The coincidence seems rather remarkable. They are identical to yours and to the samples we received very recently from the other side of the globe."

Gerry's eyes were popping out on stalks.

"That's amazing!"

For a moment his well programmed response to matters of scientific interest meant that he forgot his recent imprisonment and was back in fellow researcher mode. A sense of calm returned to him.

"You said five – there were six in the other batch?"

"Yes. And now get this; there were six in this second batch too. But only five were Hs53. The sixth is quite different."

"In what way?"

"Well I can show you the sequence, but that won't mean much to you I guess. You're here because you claimed a few days ago to have been involved with developing a search algorithm that could produce some meaningful interpretations of genetic strains such as these."

The man paused while he fixed Gerry with a very determined stare.

"The thing is Gerry, is there any remote possibility that you were telling the truth?"

Gerry's acute intellectual honesty prevented him from lying, despite the fact that not doing so would almost certainly result in his being returned to his jail.

"No, I'm afraid there isn't."

"I thought so. Nevertheless, you have spent a lot of your professional life studying this very area. We hope that you might be able to help us."

"Of course – if I can."

"I am very glad that you are being so cooperative."

It was a nice comment, though Gerry knew perfectly well that he had been softened up and manipulated.

"Here's what we do know."

The man put on his Holoviewer and passed one to Gerry. Together they explored the documentation and data relating to the two genetic samples. The man pointed to a genetic sequence in the virtual space that they shared for a moment.

"This is yours – we know that in other species this strain has led to an increase in tolerance of radiation. As you will realise, since much of the planet is already devastated by radioactive fallout, any future evolution of the human species needs to be able to live in a contaminated environment. It might be politic for us to give the process a bit of a nudge…"

"By selective breeding?"

"Yes – quite so. Now this sample, the odd one out, has a different variation at the same point in the sequence. But we haven't seen it anywhere else. That is where the research is needed."

"I'm not sure how I can help – the Hub has access to all categorised data. What can I possibly do?"

"Here? Nothing. But this sample isn't from here – it's from the East. There they don't have access to the Hub – and the Hub doesn't have access to their data. Our unofficial contacts in India – where this sample is thought to have originated – are trying to track down exactly where this came from. The chances are that there are some more interesting samples there, and even some useful research already in progress. We want you to go and work with a team there."

"OK – that sounds reasonable. When?"

"Why, have you got plans?"

Gerry smiled.

"I wish I had!"

"We'd like you to go today. Oh, and there's another human here with a similar but different variation in their DNA. We'd like her to go with you."

"Her?"

"Yes – her name is Avril. It would be company for you."

254

Gerry thought he might have detected a twinkle in the man's eye. He was escorted back to his apartment – still not knowing the man's name. No one he'd ever met before.

Chapter 87

Max was desperate to know what Carl had seen.

"What is it Carl?"

"Well," he hesitated, his mind being torn between what he was seeing and the need to speak to his audience, "first - the sample is being examined by the Smithsonian."

"I thought it had gone to MIT."

"It had – but clearly a decision has been made to transfer the research. And second, the Smithsonian is dispatching a team to India to do further research."

"Really – when?"

"Now!"

"That seems rather urgent."

"Yes – it must mean that the Hub has made some prediction about the nature of this variant that we don't know about."

Carl looked back at his holographic displays.

"Look – the Model 5 probability has just changed – it's gone up!"

It was now reading 0.39

"But surely, if there's more doubt introduced why doesn't the Hub reduce the probability of actioning model 5?"

"Presumably because it sees this variant as presenting some kind of threat. All the other eleven samples have a strain that shows increased immunity to radiation damage. And the effect of discovering those in the East was to up the probability of using model 5."

"Why would that be seen as a threat?"

David was being spokesman again. Unexpectedly Jacques offered an explanation.

"Presumably because if humans in the East were able to develop such a resistance it would make the east European radiation barrier less effective."

"Yes, and our current nuclear threat less of a credible disincentive to aggressive action against us."

Max had carried on Jacques' argument. "So it might precipitate a first strike?"

Carl responded; "But that seems crazy. It would take years, decades, for anyone there to take these strains and use them to develop an increase in resistance in the general public."

"Maybe…" Max was pulling on his imaginary beard… "maybe it's not the general public it is thinking about; rather, small numbers of spies, terrorists – people who could break through the barrier undetected, infiltrate our world, conduct espionage. And maybe they have already done this? If it's a possibility then you can be sure that the Hub has already predicted it. This new evidence increases the chance of that possibility already being real."

Max seemed agitated. His usual cool exterior had given way to a collection of creases and ticks. Carl viewed him with concern. His old friend could usually be relied upon to keep calm under the most severe of conditions. He wished he knew what was going on in Max's mind; but he couldn't ask.

"So what is the purpose of the research team going to India?" Jacques again.

It was not intended to be a rhetorical question, but nobody seemed inclined to answer it.

Chapter 88

Gerry and Avril were enjoying their luxury flight on a private long haul jet. It was a long flight so there would be plenty of time for catching up with each other's background and experience of their strange relationship. Strangely, they didn't seem particularly keen to start that conversation.

Gerry had excitedly briefed Avril on the genetic science that lay behind the Smithsonian's interest in his DNA. Avril also had some unusual genetic history, which they knew was related to her sense of smell.

"Ah – G&T – I would love one! What about you?"

"How do you know it's a G&T?"

"Oh – sorry, I can smell the tonic."

"From here?!"

"Oh yes – I've always had a good sense of smell."

"You're not kidding."

At this point Marcel, one of the science officers in the team travelling to India, came to join them.

"We had better begin your briefing. There's a lot to get through. How much do you know?"

"That depends on what you mean by 'know'."

Gerry was working up to being somewhat petulant. He had been holding onto a bucket load of resentment at his enforced imprisonment and all that emotion was looking for a suitable figure of authority on which to dump itself. Marcel seemed to be an ideal candidate – especially when he asked stupid questions like that.

"If you mean 'what have we been told'? then the answer is very little. If you mean 'what have we managed to work out for ourselves?' then it's not much more."

"Ah, yes." The man re-arranged his hair nervously.

"Well how about you tell me what you know – then I won't have to bore you unnecessarily."

Gerry appreciated the humour. He rehearsed what he had already said to Avril, about his own genetic background and its interest to science because of the existence of a historic and extinct gene sequence. Avril noticed that as Gerry got into the swing of his lecture he became excited but less stressed. She was beginning to find him interesting.

"Avril has an unusual gene sequence which produces an enhanced sense of smell and I have one which is thought to be associated with an increased resistance to radiation damage."

"Yes – that's about right. Although, in fact, Avril's gene sequence also tends to produce an increased tolerance for radiation."

Avril and Gerry looked at one another as they realised the possible reason for their both being sent on this research mission.

"And do you know about the recent discovery of new samples?"

"Yes, six from the East and six in an old archive in Washington."

"Correct. Although only five of the samples from the East are Hs53. The sixth one has a completely different gene sequence in the relevant section."

Avril was looking mystified.

"What this means," he paused for emphasis "is that we have discovered considerably more samples of Hs53 in the East than previously we had thought existed. But also that there is an altogether different variant which some institution in India has been examining along with Hs53. We are keen to find out which institution, why they have been investigating this new variant, what they have discovered about it and what use it might be to us."

"And you have no idea what the effect of this new strain might be?"

"No, none whatsoever. Though it seems likely to be very significant – otherwise they wouldn't have been researching it."

"OK, what I don't quite get is why Gerry and I are being shipped out as well."

"Ah, well, Gerry's work at the Smithsonian has been connected with comparing the natural process of human reproduction with the 'replication' process that we now use. In particular we are interested to know what impact this might have on the process of combining parent genetic material from Hs53 samples. We will be wanting to use some of your eggs and sperm for short term experiments."

Avril and Gerry nodded in understanding. They were not shocked by the revelation – experimentation on human embryos using human donors had been mainstream for decades and Avril and Gerry's naturally scientific mind-sets led them to conclude that it made perfect sense.

23:00

In the Castle Max and the other members of the group were rapidly tiring. Their nerves had been on edge all day and the clock was indicating both that this was day zero and that there was only one hour left. The probability table indicated there had been no change in the Hub's probable intention to wipe out the large majority of the world's population. It most probably wouldn't; but it might.

"This is like waiting to see if you have won the lottery!" exclaimed Jacques.

"Hardly" replied Carl. "Your chance of winning the lottery is one in several billion billion. The chance of model 5 being implemented is one in 2.5641 – approximately. Much better odds!"

The news about their improved odds did not seem to bring any cheer to the room.

"What happens if nothing happens in the next hour?"

"The thing is we don't know whether the Hub will review its strategy immediately, or later. Given that there is a team on its way to India to do more research, we might expect the Hub to decide to wait. On the other hand it might decide that the increased risk to security is best dealt with by taking pre-emptive action."

"But that would be insane!"

Jacques was clearly mad with frustration.

"Yes, insane to you and me; because we are human. And we make decisions based on emotions. The Hub makes decisions based on statistics, probabilities, logic. Which of us, for example, would have been able to kill a three week old baby if we had been told he would probably grow up to be a cruel and insane dictator? No, we would wait until it became clear. Wait until it's too late."

"But I don't believe the Hub is capable of making that kind of prediction – not with any certainty." Max was clearly very uncomfortable with the direction the conversation was going.

"That's the point. We humans look for certainty – and if we can't find it we make it up. The Hub deals only with probabilities. If there is a chance of something developing in the East that could threaten our existence and the preservation of our genetic inheritance, and killing off six billion people in the East would probably prevent that, then it's probably a good course of action

261

to take. If the decision is wrong, so what; people are very good at re-populating the world!"

Max raised his arm slowly indicating that a deduction had made itself in his mind.

"And if that re-population has to happen in an irradiated environment, you need a strain of gene that is more resistant to radiation!"

Carl remained perfectly calm.

"Yes – so the result of this further research in India is going to be very interesting to the Hub – therefore I think the likelihood of model 5 being implemented is actually very low – for the time being."

"I don't agree. Why hasn't the probability table indicated that?"

Max was beginning to get agitated. No one had ever seen him this agitated before. David rose to his feet;

"What would you propose doing Max?"

"I think we have no choice. *We* have to remove the chance of the Hub carrying out that action – pre-emptively."

"And just how do we do that?" Carl shot a sharp look at Max. Suddenly he felt he was not in control.

"I think we need to communicate with the Hub, directly."

Max had suggested what seemed like a reasonable proposal. Jacques was mystified.

"So why haven't we done that before?"

Chapter 89

"So, any questions?"

Marcel had been going over fine detail for some time now. Gerry's question was somewhat obscure but it had been at the back of his mind for some time.

"Where are the samples? – on board this plane?"

"Oh, goodness me, no! There are four known samples in the West. Then there are the eleven that have appeared in the last few days. And then there's you two. We are hardly likely to put all our eggs in one basket are we!"

"Where are they then?"

"There are two batches of six samples in separate planes, using different routes. The other four remain wherever they have been."

"Even so, is it wise to have 14 out of 18 samples all out of our region at once?"

Marcel eyed Gerry cautiously.

"Well you might ask. Precautions have been taken."

Marcel was smiling. His seat allowed him to look towards the rear of the plane and, therefore, through the window; he could see two of the four fighter jets accompanying them. Neither Gerry nor Avril could see them – they were positioned so that they could only see forward. Marcel pointed through the window. Gerry and Avril turned around and peered out.

"Oh, I see!"

"Yes my friend. You are now VVIPS!"

Avril's head was now very close to Gerry's as she strained to see out of the window. They exchanged a smile. Avril noticed a small amount of turbulence.

Chapter 90

Max was getting madder by the minute. David intervened in the discussion. He wasn't sure that he agreed with Max's reasoning. But, there again, he didn't like the way Carl's thoughts were clearly going either.

"Gentlemen, I think we need to remain calm. Carl is right to remind us that the Hub has been unbelievably successful in maintaining peace in the West – for decades. We would be very foolish to suddenly decide that it is now incompetent."

"But haven't we already made that decision – by tampering with the Prime Directives and artificially changing the record of archived DNA samples?"

"Not quite Max. We have left the Hub completely alone in terms of its structure. Those samples existed before – they merely hadn't been discovered before. As for the Prime Directives, they are essentially the human interface to the Hub. They contain the value structure that a machine cannot create for itself. All we did was to acknowledge that we ourselves had set that up slightly wrong."

Max did not look convinced. Nor did he seem to be relaxing. In fact, the veins on his forehead were enlarged and visibly pumping. He was getting fidgety and agitated. After a few moments he uttered a shout.

"This is insane – we cannot stand by here, in this isolated bunker, hoping that the inevitable isn't going to happen!"

"So what do you suggest?" David still had hopes that Max would calm down and return to rationality.

"I believe we have no choice – we simply must interrogate the Hub."

Carl turned his gaze from his holographic circus, towards Max, his hands now defiantly on his hips.

"Let me remind you of the protocols."

"Oh, bugger the protocols!"

"Unfortunately we can't do that. We have this holographic reporting tool here under our credentials as the anonymous Zurich group. As far as the world and the Hub are concerned we don't exist. However, we are permitted to read off data. We use various measures to preserve our anonymity – which is essential to our being able to continue to function as the most influential group of people in the world – well this world anyway. But we do not have the access rights to enable us to interrogate the Hub – that is, to enter into an exchange of data that could result in a change of the Hub's strategy."

"Dammit Carl – I do!"

"Yes Max *you* do – as Max Brunner. So do I – as Carl Fische. But not as anonymous members of this group. For you or me to enter into a conversation with the Hub – and have any hope of altering its strategy, we would have to disclose our true identity. Then the existence of the Zurich Group would be discoverable."

David put up a hand to add a question.

"So, are you are saying that in order to save the East we have to sacrifice our own existence as an influential group?"

"I think, ultimately, it would be the end of the Zurich group altogether."

"Well I think that may be a sacrifice we have to make!"

Carl eyed Max through slitted eyes, as if he couldn't quite believe what he was hearing and seeing. The intensity of their penetrating blue was sharply focussed.

"Max – are you turning traitor?" His words were slow and measured.

Suddenly all eyes in the room were on Max. He was chewing the inside of his lip, his normal calm exterior clearly shattered. The clock on the wall indicated there were five minutes left before the end of a very long Sunday.

Chapter 91

It would be another eight hours or so before Avril and Gerry touched down in Delhi. At the same time the other twelve genetic samples would land at two separate military airports in India. In various universities across the country, academics and scientists were meeting with security officials and plans were being made for the safe delivery of the samples. Other scientists were hastily putting together research plans. There was no little excitement at the prospect of such a promising set of new experimental data being discovered.

Whatever life lay ahead for Gerry and Avril, it was certainly going to be very different from the one they had just left. Gerry's expression revealed little of the emotions he was feeling. But Avril noticed the recurring twitch in his eye.

Chapter 92

Max dropped his stare. Something seemed to switch in his mind. It was as if suddenly there was no one else in the room. He muttered something incomprehensible, turned on his heel and walked out of the room.

"Where is he going?" Jacques asked.

"I don't know – I'm going to see."

Carl was close behind him, his long legs quickly getting into a huge, if rather ungainly stride. Once into the long corridor, Carl broke into a run. Max already had fifty yards on him. The chase continued up a staircase. Max deftly worked his way through the automatic barrier gates, using his Vector. Carl did the same. Within seconds they had emerged into the bright moonlit Swiss night.

Max was standing with his back towards Carl. He seemed to be talking to someone. Carl couldn't quite work out what he was saying. He inched closer, trying not to make a sound. Gradually a few syllables became recognisable. He thought he heard the name 'Jennifer'. A shiver went down his spine. An image came back to him – from decades before.

He had been sailing with his girlfriend – now so long lost in the past that he couldn't remember her name. Max was on the helm. It was midnight and the moon was full, just touching the horizon. Max's girlfriend, Jennifer, was standing at the bow, her long hair waving in the breeze. Clearly she was lost in the romance of the moment. The four friends had been to France for a week and were making their way back to the Solent. They had about five hours' sailing ahead of them. There was little wind but they weren't in a hurry. The dim navigation lights of a few other vessels could be seen in the distance ahead.

Carl had announced his intention to put a position on the chart. Jennifer came aft to take the helm while Carl and Max went below to attend to the chart-work. Carl's girlfriend was asleep in the quarter birth. The two men talked quietly about their speed, the tides, their ETA. Suddenly Max looked up. "Listen!" he had said. "What? I can't hear anything." "Exactly – it's too quiet." They both made quickly for the deck. The cockpit was empty. The tiller had been lashed in place to keep the boat on course. The deck was empty too.

Carl shuddered as he recalled the moments of panic, the seemingly unending period of searching, the Mayday call and the slow realisation that whatever Jennifer's last thoughts had been they clearly weren't the romantic ones that Max had hoped for.

Everyone thought Max had done well to eventually cope with the grief. But Carl wondered if he had only suppressed it all. Now he knew.

Max turned, his silver hair iridescent in the moonlight.

"What are you doing Max?"

"It's already done, Carl." Max was calm yet also clearly stressed.

"What do you mean?"

"Where is your scarf?"

Carl put his hand to his neck. But he already knew the instant Max asked the question; his scarf was still inside. So was Max's.

"My God Max. You've blown our cover!"

"Yes. Now we can communicate with the Hub."

Max looked triumphant. He was about to start the nearest thing one could get to a conversation with the Hub and had high hopes of being able to change its mind.

Carl stood in silence, his face drained of all expression. He stared at Max with incredulity. It seemed that his old and dear friend had suddenly lost all contact with reality. David and Jacques emerged from the Castle and stood with them. They also had forgotten to think about their scarves. On a cold mountain in Switzerland the four most powerful, secretive, men on earth stood un-masked.

Chapter 93

A mile to the east a security drone took off. It was about one metre in diameter. It was controlled by the security section of the Hub's all pervasive system. It flew the short distance at a speed slightly over fifty miles per hour. Within a little over a minute it appeared over the four men and hovered. Four rapid laser blasts silently found their targets on the men's heads. The Zurich group was no more.

In the Control room which the four had so recently deserted, Carl's holographic circus was still active. A servant came in to clear up the cups. She gave it a cursory glance, but it all meant nothing to her. She didn't even notice the Janet and John display, the probability table. If she had, she would have seen that the number against 'Model 5' had dropped from 0.39 to zero.

Chapter 94

Gerry and Avril walked out of the plane and into the dry oven-like air of New Delhi's late afternoon. Marcel stood behind them as they viewed their new world. Gerry was under no illusions about ever being allowed back to his homeland. And after the experience of the past few weeks, being changed from scientist to the object of scientific research, he wasn't sure that he would ever want to.

"Well, we can't stand here for ever you know!"

Marcel was clearly keen to get on with the next chapter of his far less complex life. Avril, meanwhile, had turned her face towards the sun and was clearly in the moment. An airport staff member walked across the tarmac to greet them.

"We will have your luggage sorted out as soon as we can."

The man was earnest and clearly keen to be helpful.

"They'll have fun trying to find ours!" Gerry commented to Avril.

"What a wonderful country!" she said, ignoring the luggage problem altogether.

"Please follow me."

They were led through a side door, avoiding customs, and once inside the VIP lounge were met by a member of India's civil service.

"This is Meeta", the staff member turned "Avril and Gerry."

Meeta extended a hand to welcome them.

"Welcome to India. We have been looking forward to your arrival. My boss is very excited to meet you soon."

"Thank you for your welcome Meeta. Who is your boss?"

"Oh he is a very important person here in India, his name is Aditya. He is the head of our civil service"

The name meant nothing to Gerry or Avril.

"I am sure we are very honoured – but why would he want to meet us?"

"You will have to ask *him* that question!"

So far they had been assiduously accompanied by Meeta. Gerry assumed she was an important part of the research team.

"Have the Hs53 samples arrived yet?"

Meeta looked puzzled.

"I'm sorry, but I don't know what you mean. What is Hs53?"

Marcel leant confidentially over to Gerry and whispered;

"I think it's beyond her pay-grade to know about that."

The three smiled conspiratorially. They were led out of the airport and into a black limousine. As they sped away, they were accompanied by unmarked black outriders. Gerry was beginning to feel less welcome and more anxious.

"Where are we going?"

Meeta replied with a slightly patronising smile.

"We are going to meet Aditya. So all your questions can be answered soon."

Chapter 95

Eddie was enjoying a whiskey as he relaxed. It was early morning and he could see his ranch extending out far ahead of him. He enjoyed retirement and was glad to have little to do except receive daily reports of his increasing profits. Oil had been good to his family in the past and clearly hydrogen was going to be even better to it in the future. A soft buzzing sound interrupted his meditation. It was his Vector. He hadn't been troubled by it for several weeks now – he had asked Max to give him a bit of a break. Max had been more than happy to oblige. Eddie cursed and took the device out of his pocket.

"Code 9 alert. Attend Zurich immediately."

He was damned if he could remember what a 'code 9' was. He'd have to look it up.

Back in the house he began rummaging through his papers in his desk. All information relating to the Zurich group was only ever committed to paper. You never spoke about it outside of the group, or referred to it in any electronic communication.

"Ah – here's the damn list."

He ran his index finger down the list until he got to '9'. When he read it his whiskey glass fell from his hand.

Andrew Barrington had been having lunch when his Vector buzzed gently. He had been aware that something serious was happening and had hoped until now that no news was good news. When he saw 'code 9' he knew only too well what it meant. There was a serious leadership problem. Somebody must have died or become permanently absent. His thoughts naturally turned to trying to guess who it was. The most likely candidate was David Carsons – he was the oldest of the group and had worked with Andrew's father, Simon. However, it might not have been age that had now claimed another victim. With Aditya being in India there was always the chance of a terrorist act – or worse. He quickly left his family at the table, picked up his overnight ready bag and got into his car to be taken to the airport. He would arrive at Glanzenberg Castle within a couple of hours.

Meanwhile in New Delhi, Aditya was thinking through a wholly different range of possibilities in response to his code 9. He alone among the remaining leading members of the Zurich group knew what had been going on. The last message he had received from Max indicated that all was not quite going to plan. The risk of Model 5 being implemented by the Hub had not fallen, even when the second set of samples had arrived in Washington. Consequently, he was not exactly expecting good news!

But he wasn't expecting a code 9. If one of the four at Zurich had been killed then all sorts of possibilities would come to mind. It was going to take him eight hours to get to the Castle. He couldn't wait that long to know what was going on. He tried to raise Max on the Vector but without success. Then he tried Carl. When that attempt failed he began to feel depressed. By the time he had tried David without any reply he gave up hope of anything better from Jacques.

He called his secretary to cancel his meetings for the next three days and set off for Zurich. It would take him as long to get to the private jet that was going to smuggle him out of India as the flight to Zurich would take. Although his status within the Civil Service would give him the right to travel to any country in the West, he wasn't going as India's senior civil servant; he was travelling as one of seven, wholly secret, members of a very secret group of people – whose identities were as unknown as their influence was unseen. He just hoped that Max would be able to organise one of his ex-Vatican Swiss Guards at the other end.

Chapter 96

The limousine raced through the city and arrived at its destination far sooner than Gerry had expected – not that he had any reason to be able to estimate the journey time; he didn't know where they were going. The destination was a very large and beautiful government building, the Rashtrapati Bhavan, built by the British in 1910 and later used as the President's house. They had a short walk to a side door and were led inside to a waiting room. Their guide disappeared for a moment before returning to give them bad news.

"I'm terribly sorry but your meeting will have to be delayed until next week.

Meeta was covered in embarrassment.

"I am so sorry – I can't think what has happened - but it must be something very urgent to take the head of the civil service away like this."

For Gerry and Avril it was a matter of little consequence since they did not really know why they were there in the first place. One thing at least it guaranteed – they wouldn't be going back for over a week.

It was, however, a very grand welcome to the new continent.

Chapter 97

The first of the three to arrive at Glanzenberg was Andrew Barrington. From the airport he took a taxi to Zurich. Then he walked the remaining mile to the castle. The automatic security door opened silently for him. A soulless voice welcomed him. Inside he was greeted by one of the staff who as usual offered him tea. Inside the inner sanctum Andrew was shocked by what he saw.

Carl's 3d holographic display was still operating. The images were quite meaningless to Andrew and there was no sign of Carl. He called out –

"Carl? Max? David? Jacques?"

The room seemed to have been abandoned right in the middle of a meeting. There was nothing else there to indicate whether there had been people in the room recently or not. Just the display. Andrew waited. Andrew drank tea. Andrew bit his nails. Andrew was not a patient man ... Finally a sound in the corridor made him jump. When Ed walked through the door he couldn't believe his eyes.

"Ed! – what are you doing here?"

"Gee, don't ask me. Same as you. Answering the call."

"Where is everybody?"

"I haven't seen anyone – except you. Who are you expecting?"

"Well I don't know. I thought Max and Carl would be here at least. Or David or Jacques. I know the four were here yesterday."

"OK – I've been out of the loop for a while. Asked not to be disturbed. Then I get this code 9 thing – had to go and look it up!"

They both spent a while looking at Carl's creation but with no further illumination. Andrew tried his Vector once again. Still no response from anyone whom he had been sure were present the previous day.

Vector had some automated processes – like that one that had issued the code 9 alert when the other four had failed to respond to previous messages. But it lacked the intelligence of the Hub, so there was little they could do but wait. The code 9 would have been issued to the remaining members of the ruling elite of the Zurich group. Vector would have logged their responses and would issue further information once they had all arrived, or sent their apologies. This protocol was intended to ensure that no 'conclusion' could be arrived at unless the group was gathered together.

Chapter 98

Aditya's plane landed at Zurich on time. He was dressed as a pilot – a legend that gave him a reasonably wide range of options. The flight was a private charter, allegedly empty on the inbound journey but returning with a political attaché. There was no political attaché, of course, but it enabled the correct boxes to be ticked. After a few hours the attaché would be declared a 'no-show' and the plane would return empty.

Meanwhile Aditya successfully outwitted the security guards and walked out into the entrance area, vainly looking for someone who looked like a retired Vatican Swiss guard. Aditya had been to the Castle before, of course, but always in a car. And he had never paid enough attention to the route to be able to replicate it. A journey in a car was always an ideal opportunity for some more thinking. It wasn't a place you could ask directions to – officially it didn't exist. It was just a derelict old castle. And Aditya certainly couldn't ask the way to a derelict castle looking like an airplane pilot!

He tried to contact Max on Vector but again without success. He decided to start walking. He knew that it was only a mile or so from Zurich but it would be about three hours walk from the airport. He tried to recall the last time he had been. Eventually he remembered an area in the City that he had travelled through.

He abandoned his hat and tie, rolled up his sleeves and tried to look a bit less obvious. Without a PIDAC of course he was unable to get a taxi to serve him. He resigned himself to a long run.

*****

As the ruin came in sight it looked familiar, although he was coming at it from a different direction. As he came within a hundred yards of the Castle entrance what he saw horrified him.

Chapter 99

From the luxurious Presidential palace that Gerry had briefly glimpsed, they were transferred to their temporary accommodation in a down-town hotel. The three of them had adjacent rooms and were served dinner in their rooms. Afterwards they met up in Gerry's room for a drink and an attempt to work out what was happening.

Marcel knew there were some samples of Hs53 arriving in Delhi from Washington. He didn't yet know that only a few days before, they had left Delhi in the other direction. Neither did he know the torturous and highly risky journeys the samples had taken. However, he did know that Gerry and Avril were embodiments of this rare gene and that Gerry, coincidentally, was a brilliant geneticist. He also knew that Gerry had been working on a project that was highly germane to the research into Hs53 that had been Marcus' meat and drink for years. However he didn't know that Gerry had made that bit up!

"So, Avril, I think I know what Gerry's role here is going to be. But what about you?"

"I'm as confused as you are. I know that I also have the rare Hs53 gene but my work was not related to that at all."

"What was it?"

"Legal – I used to double check court judgements issued by the Hub."

"Did they need double checking? I thought it was practically faultless."

"Yes it is. But some processes require legal protocols to be followed and that was what I did."

"Anything interesting?"

"Sometimes – but the most interesting was when I had to check the very document that demoted me from being a free citizen to being a zoological sample!"

"What an extraordinary coincidence – and how horrifying!"

"The other intriguing thing is that my genetic variation seems to have another side-effect."

"Which is?"

"An abnormal sense of smell!"

"Really – what can you smell?"

"Anything that you can smell but in minute quantities. So, if you can smell a rose 5 centimetres away I can smell it 50 metres away."

"Sounds terrible!"

"It can be – but you zone it out after a while."

"Wow – did you smell anything on the flight?"

"Yes – loads of things – some good some bad. Actually one very strange smell – as we came over the DMZ."

DMZ – demilitarised zone – was still the term people used to describe the irradiated thousand mile long strip of Europe between the West and the East. No one had ever come up with a more imaginative name.

"Perhaps you could smell the radiation!"

They laughed - but Marcel's words hung in the air.

Chapter 100

Aditya had come over a slight mound in the earth. Behind it, out of sight to any casual visitor – not that there were many of those now – he saw what looked like four people lying asleep on the grass. As he got closer he realised that this was exactly what they were. However, they were not sleeping – their eyes were staring open. As he approached he recognised their faces and, with horror, saw the holes bored into their skulls by the drone-born laser.

He ran into the building using his Vector to gain access. In the secure meeting room, where he had expected to find at least some of the people whose corpses now lay outside in the grass, he found Eddie and Andrew. They turned to look at him. What they saw was not just another unexpected face; but a face drained of all colour.

"What's happened?" Andrew asked.

"Have you seen what's outside?"

"What do you mean?"

"The others – Max, Carl, Jacques, David – they're all dead!"

"What!" Eddie yelled, starting to run towards the door.

"Stop! You can't go outside!"

"Why not?"

"Think about it – they were all killed – laser beams to the head. They've each got a perfect 15mm diameter hole in the top of their skull. Whatever did that to them might well do it to you too."

"Or you!"

"Probably not. I don't have a PIDAC – remember."

This observation brought a sudden and deep numbing to the other two men. They all recognised the method of execution. It was the Hub's hallmark. It was very seldom necessary for the Hub to actually execute anyone. Normally deactivation was enough to bring people to heel. But occasionally it deemed it necessary to eliminate someone presenting a severe threat – potential terrorists or spies, for example.

Andrew broke the silence.

"We all know who – or rather what – did this. The question is why?"

"From what I understand of your Hub system there is no way of forcing it to reveal information about its decision making."

"That's right. It's like a gigantic mind that's distributed across billions of computers and chips, all across the West. You can peek inside any one of them but it won't show you what it's thinking."

"Is there any way of asking it?"

"Sounds a dumb idea to me!"

"No, Aditya has a good question. But the answer is no. At least none of *us* can. To do so you'd have to be known to the Hub. Aditya doesn't have a PIDAC so it won't recognise him. We do have PIDACs but if we go out of this radio-wave proof chamber it will know that we are members of the Zurich group and presumably treat us the same way as them."

"What about the scarves?" Ed asked.

"Well yes we can wear them – but then it won't recognise us either."

"Even if we did manage to establish a link it probably won't reveal its strategic planning – it doesn't have an equivalent to our consciousness with which to formulate such opinions." Andrew was going slightly beyond his audience's understanding.

"So, what *do* we know?" Andrew started accumulating information.

"We know that four members of the Zurich group were here yesterday. However, we don't know what they were doing, do we?"

"Yes – well I do." Aditya offered some insight. "They were monitoring a change to one of the PDs."

"Oh that!" said Ed dismissively.

"Which ones?" asked Andrew.

"Just the one actually. It's to do with the value placed on genetic variants in historical DNA samples. It was hoped that by increasing this value, the Hub could be induced to give more weight to the needs of the East."

"How would that work?"

"Let me explain Andrew; the Hub seemed to be on the brink of possibly wiping out the whole of the Eastern world. It was deemed no longer necessary for resources and the increase in terrorist behaviour and its consumption of resources was becoming a threat to the West."

"But that's crazy!" Andrew was visibly aghast. "That would run counter to the fundamental PD to protect human life!"

"No, actually; it's *valid* human life it has to protect. The Eastern populations are not considered valid."

"How long have you known this Aditya?"

Aditya gave Andrew a blank look. "Far too long. Anyway, hence the attempt to change the balance."

"Why not just make humans in the East '*valid*'?"

"You have to remember where this all started. A nuclear world war and unrestrained immigration. The planet cannot sustain 8 billion people. In any case, you can't be valid without a PIDAC!"

"Who dreamt up this stuff anyway?" Ed was revealing his contempt.

"Our predecessors – who created the Hub."

Aditya was being deliberately vague. He knew that apart from himself the other authors of the Hub lay silent on the grass outside.

"And as long as the East was not too badly behaved *and* while the West needed priceless resources like coal, oil and gas – it all worked well."

"So, let me see if I have got this right. Max and the others were implementing a change in the moral foundation of the Hub in order to save the lives of 6 billion people?"

"That's about it Andrew."

"And I wasn't informed…"

"This has never been a democracy Andrew – and you know the rule. Only those who come, know."

Aditya let the thoughts sink in for a while before he started again.

"And there's more. We identified some samples of an ancient human genetic variant – Hs53. We knew there were a few examples here in the West. But we also found a dozen samples in the East. By implanting those samples in our archive in Washington we hoped to convince the Hub that the East had a significant valuable gene pool that should be protected."

"Will it work?"

"I think it already has. If you look at this display, there appears to be a table showing the likelihood of each of five possible plans of action being carried out. Model 5 – the destruction of the East – shows probability zero."

Aditya had been eyeing the holographic display for sometime, multi-tasking as usual.

"So what do we do now?" Ed was clearly getting over the emotional shock with customary rapidity and would soon be ready to go home.

"First we have to replace not one but four members of the group's command structure. Then we need to try and fathom out just what is going on. *And* – we have to work out a way of getting out of here without being identified by the Hub! Currently it seems we can either be identified and have some chance of influencing the Hub, but run the risk of being assassinated; or, we escape with our lives and abandon the Zurich group."

It seemed a pretty bleak choice.

"What's this?" Andrew was pointing to a world map which formed part of Carl's holographic circus. Aditya looked for a moment.

"I think I know. You see the red coloured spots. There are four here in the US" – he was pointing now – "and fourteen here in Delhi."

"What does that mean? What are they?" Andrew asked.

"Oh goodness me! This morning I was supposed to meet two people who had been brought from the US to Delhi. They are examples of Hs53. And in the past few days another twelve samples of Hs53 genetic material have appeared in Delhi."

"Where from?"

"From the United States."

Aditya was manipulating the graph.

"But look – before that they came from India. They're the samples we found and planted in the Washington archive. They've been sent back!"

"What does it mean?"

"I'm not sure – but coupled with the assassination of four of our group, it doesn't look good. The transfer of those human samples and the DNA samples back to the East must have been done at least with the Hub's knowledge – if not under its control. As were the assassinations. It's beginning to look like it's all part of a plan."

"What's so special about Hs53 anyway?" Ed again.

"People with that particular gene seem to have an increased tolerance for radiation. It looks like someone in the East is thinking about developing living humans with radiation resistance."

"What good would that do them?" Ed never doubted the efficacy of the DMZ.

"Well it would at least provide a supply of terrorists who could pass through the DMZ into the West – without our even suspecting it."

Andrew looked pensive, holding his chin. His eyes revolved slowly as if he were considering various other factors.

Chapter 101

The next day, Gerry, Avril and Marcel were escorted once more by Meeta, this time to a military laboratory. Once more the outriders accompanied them and barriers were flung open with what Gerry considered to be undue haste.

Once inside the complex Avril and Gerry were subjected to a range of tests, while Marcel seemed to have disappeared. He returned an hour later with a short, stocky uniformed man who was clearly very much in charge.

"Avril, Gerry – welcome to India…" he said this with a feint wave, dismissing the superficial gesture of a welcome.

"As you know you are bearers of an ancient DNA variant which is associated with an enhanced tolerance for radiation. Along with yourselves we also have a number of samples of human DNA with the same variant."

"Yes, fourteen of them."

"Well, actually thirteen. The fourteenth has a different signature again. What it seems to share with you Avril, is a propensity for a greatly enhanced sense of smell."

"Why would you be interested in that?"

"Let me ask you Avril. Did you smell anything unusual on your journey?"

Avril looked at Gerry. They were both visibly shocked.

At this point, as if on cue, Marcel re-appeared.

"Have you been briefed?"

"Partly" said Gerry. "I guess we've been told what. You want us for a genetic engineering programme to develop humans who are resistant to radiation. Right?"

"Yes – bang on."

"But what about smelling radiation? – surely that's impossible?"

"Strictly speaking, yes. No one could smell alpha, beta or gamma particles but, to a greater or lesser degree, they tend to ionise other atoms. That is what you detected flying over the DMZ Avril."

"That's amazing!" Gerry's eyes were wide open and flickering around as his thought processes accelerated. No wonder you wanted the two of us!"

He paused, as if to compartmentalise this new piece of information, before continuing with his previous answer.

"But we don't know why."

"Ah – let me explain. The research here is funded by the military in India. But it's a covert operation – officially it's not happening. But there is also an input from the West – from Washington, Smithsonian in particular; though we guess that's a cover for the US government."

"If you don't mind my saying so that doesn't make sense." Avril was trying to understand the logic. "If it's a joint project between the US and India, how does that fit in with the Hub's Prime Directives?"

"To be frank we don't know. Since it's hush-hush at both ends no one can give us a proper answer."

"So it might not be a joint venture at all?"

"You're right it might not."

"In fact" said Gerry "it might not be directed by either government?"

Chapter 102

"So, Aditya, why were you meeting these Americans this morning?"

"It's a good question Ed. I was told that the man – Gerry – has a unique algorithm for doing DNA searches – it would speed up genetic research by a factor of ten or more."

"Who told you that?"

"It was in the file that came across last week."

"Which file?"

"It came from the central repository."

The central repository was just a name really – there was no longer anything central about it. All the information it held was in distributed computer memory. But, if the information was in CR, then it was more or less for public consumption. Organisations, governments, universities, individuals with special privileges – all of these categories could lodge documents there.

"Who authorised it?" Andrew was determined to get to the root of this.

"The source was not declared - which is very unusual. In fact the only time the source is marked undeclared – usually – is when it's lodged by the Hub."

"So let me get this right." Ed was still visibly impatient. "The Hub has captured 14 samples of DNA, two in living human beings, transported them halfway across the planet to India, whilst making it public that one of the human sources has some special and unique expertise in genetic engineering. Why the hell would it do that?"

There was a long pause before Aditya came out of what looked like a trance.

"I can think of several reasons. Although the problem with second guessing the hub is that we don't really know how, or what, it thinks. Human beings have evolved to be communicators. They can tell each other what they are thinking, why they make the decisions they make. That allows them to negotiate, argue, bargain with each other. Plus they all have more or less equivalent levels of intelligence. The hub is not like that."

"What do you mean?"

"Well, first, it has no need to communicate its reasoning – indeed it doesn't have anything resembling human consciousness, so it can't be reflective. This was deliberate. If it had been given that facility it would be open to manipulation – which leads down the murky road of politics. And we all know where that leads!"

Ed wasn't sure whether this was meant to be a joke or not so he simply nodded in agreement.

"Secondly, its processing powers far exceed those of a human brain by several orders of magnitude. So, even if it were able to communicate, we probably wouldn't have a clue what it was on about."

Ed was well acquainted with that situation.

"I thought you said you could think of several reasons for the Hub transporting the samples to India – but now you're saying we can't possibly understand it anyway."

"That's about the sum of it. I can think of reasons why a human might behave this way. But as for the Hub, speculation would be merely guesswork."

"So, can you think of any reasons or not?"

"Only one feasible one."

Chapter 103

Simultaneously in Moscow and Beijing the foreign ministers were summoned to a top level meeting with their Presidents.

Guowei Xu had arrived flustered. His family were about to celebrate his birthday and the call from his office had been as unwelcome as it was urgent. Had he lingered he would have been in trouble with the President – and no one wants that. Had he rushed away he would be in trouble with his wife – an equally unpleasant fate. Consequently Guowei dithered and panicked. It seemed he was likely to be unpopular with both. On the way to the Presidential office, Guowei reflected on the irony that apparently great power and high status came with a life of servitude and obsequiousness. Whatever this top priority meeting was about it was certainly not going to make his life easier.

The President, on the other hand, was supremely relaxed. He had never personally received a message from IDIC before and he assumed it meant that the West was in trouble. He had yet to read the message – it was in an encrypted format which meant that his secretary could only read the subject and not the content and therefore could only advise him of the subject. She had routinely interpreted the subject as meaning that an urgent meeting of the President and foreign minister was essential. It was all there in the rule book.

The President had rung his hands with anticipation when he first received his secretary's call. The West had, in terms of international politics, remained very silent for many years now. He and his colleagues firmly believed that the '*post-capitalist robot government*', as he called it, was bound to fail. His government had invested heavily in various attempts to infiltrate the Hub, but without any success.

On the other hand China's Ministry of State Security had failed to detect a single attempt on the part of the Hub to penetrate their own computer systems. It was as if the Hub had been simply ignoring them. Now, it seemed, things were about to change.

Meanwhile, in the Senate Building in the Kremlin, Guowei's counterpart Annushka Lavrov, had arrived early. A ruthless former foreign ambassador, with no scruples about disappointing anyone, let alone her family, Annushka was single-minded and absolutely determined. Her President was weak and easily manipulated, which was the principle reason for her prompt attendance at meetings involving the President. It was imperative that she got first shot at influencing the outcome of the meeting. She had already read and re-read the message from IDIC. Nothing in her previous experience or training could have prepared her for what she was now reading. In fact she was 90 percent certain that it was a hoax. She summoned an officer from the Foreign Intelligence Service to get the validity of the message double-checked. At the same time she put through a call to Guowei, since she had seen his name on the list of addressees of the message. By now, Guowei had arrived at the Presidential office, relieved to find that his President was late. The two foreign ministers therefore had an unexpected opportunity for a private conversation.

"Guowei, what do you make of this message? Do you think it's authentic?"

There was silence from the other end. This was not surprising since Guowei had only read the decrypted message that very instant and was in a state of shock.

"Just a moment Annushka. I need to read this again. It seems to be a ridiculous threat; but our people believe it is authentic."

Chapter 104

In Zurich all eyes in the room were fixed on the Janet and John display. Aditya's last words were hanging in the air, no longer attracting any attention. Model 5 probability was no longer zero. It had risen to 4.

"What the hell is happening?" yelled Ed.

"Looks like your tin dictator has changed its awesome mind." Andrew's words and face both dripped with sarcasm.

Aditya looked stony faced and was silent.

"What do you think Aditya?" Andrew asked.

Aditya raised his eyebrows and shook his face, as if being drawn out of a troublesome and captivating dream.

"I think," he paused, measuring his words; "I think it is now impossible to even guess what is in the Hub's mind. We have no clue as to what its strategy is."

Andrew's comms device sprung into life. Shortly he was talking to his colleagues at MI6. It was a short conversation and mostly one sided. Andrew's face dropped as his listened.

"Gentlemen" he addressed the group. "My people have intercepted some communication between IDIC and the Presidents of Russia and China."

He paused, not only to let his words sink in, but also because the import of them was only just registering in his own mind.

"Do you know what the content is?"

"No Aditya, we haven't been able to decrypt it. But for there to be a top level communication between the Hub and the leading powers of the East, at the same time as we see the probability of a holocaustic attack on the East, suggests that some kind of deal is being offered."

"That could be good news?"

Aditya was desperately looking for a silver lining to the cloud that hung over his relatives, friends and compatriots.

Chapter 105

In Moscow and Beijing the agenda of both meetings was virtually identical. A message had been received from IDIC. It was the body that theoretically had oversight of the Hub. In practice it was the nearest the Hub had to a mouthpiece.

Russia and China, remaining part of the East politically and practically, were not usually party to communications from IDIC.

The message read;

> *Today it has become apparent that the Eastern nations have in their possession the necessary resources for conducting a human genetic engineering programme that will give them a significant advantage in any future nuclear engagement. Accordingly a preventative plan is in place to remove this threat through the complete eradication of the Eastern nations.*
>
> *There is, however, an alternative. If the governments of Russia and China will agree to the following conditions then the eradication order will be rescinded*
>
> 1. *Implantation of PIDACs is to be implemented in all their populations.*
> 2. *They will enforce the same in the other Eastern nations.*
> 3. *Together with the implantation programme, a programme of interconnection of all intelligent devices, as has been implemented in the West, will also be started.*
> 4. *Finally the two super powers will begin a programme of population control that will reduce the total population of the East to two billion within five years.*
>
> *You have twenty four hours to respond.*

The two Presidents, separated by over three thousand miles, both crumpled at the same moment. Guowei tried to find words to reassure his President. Annushka was more pragmatic; "Mr President, we have no choice but to acquiesce."